The Blue Lady of Coffin Hall

Read all the mysteries in the

NANCY DREW DIARIES

#1 Curse of the *Arctic Star*

#2 Strangers on a Train

#3 Mystery of the Midnight Rider

#4 Once Upon a Thriller

#5 Sabotage at Willow Woods

#6 Secret at Mystic Lake

#7 The Phantom of Nantucket

#8 The Magician's Secret

#9 The Clue at Black Creek Farm

#10 A Script for Danger

#11 The Red Slippers

#12 The Sign in the Smoke

#13 The Ghost of Grey Fox Inn

#14 Riverboat Roulette

#15 The Professor and the Puzzle

#16 The Haunting on Heliotrope Lane

A Nancy Drew Christmas

#17 Famous Mistakes

#18 The Stolen Show

#19 Hidden Pictures

#20 The Vanishing Statue

#21 Danger at the Iron Dragon

#22 A Capitol Crime

Coming soon:

#24 Captain Stone's Revenge

NANCY DREW DIARIES™

The Blue Lady of Coffin Hall

#23

CAROLYN KEENE

NEW YORK   LONDON   TORONTO   SYDNEY   NEW DELHI

ALADDIN

An imprint of Simon & Schuster Children's Publishing Division
1230 Avenue of the Americas, New York, New York 10020
First Aladdin hardcover edition January 2022
Text copyright © 2022 by Simon & Schuster, Inc.
Jacket illustration copyright © 2022 by Erin McGuire
Also available in an Aladdin paperback edition.

For information about special discounts for bulk purchases, please contact
Simon & Schuster Special Sales at 1-866-506-1949 or business@simonandschuster.com.
The Simon & Schuster Speakers Bureau can bring authors to your live event.
For more information or to book an event contact the Simon & Schuster Speakers Bureau
at 1-866-248-3049 or visit our website at www.simonspeakers.com.
Series designed by Karin Paprocki
Jacket designed by Alicia Mikles
Interior designed by Mike Rosamilia
The text of this book was set in Adobe Caslon Pro.
Manufactured in the United States of America 1121 FFG
2 4 6 8 10 9 7 5 3 1
Library of Congress Cataloging-in-Publication Data
Names: Keene, Carolyn, author.
Title: The Blue Lady of Coffin Hall / Carolyn Keene.
Description: First Aladdin edition. | New York : Aladdin, 2022. | Series: Nancy Drew diaries ; 23 |
Audience: Ages 8 to 12. | Summary: Nancy and her boyfriend, Ned, visit Coffin Hall to research the library's
rumored ghost, but when a fire breaks out and Ned is blamed, it is up to Nancy to find the true culprit.
Identifiers: LCCN 2021026226 (print) | LCCN 2021026227 (ebook) |
ISBN 9781534461383 (hardcover) | ISBN 9781534461376 (paperback) | ISBN 9781534461390 (ebook)
Subjects: CYAC: Ghosts—Fiction. | Arson—Fiction. | Mystery and detective stories. | LCGFT: Novels.
Classification: LCC PZ7.K23 Bl 2022 (print) | LCC PZ7.K23 (ebook) |
DDC [Fic]—dc23
LC record available at https://lccn.loc.gov/2021026226
LC ebook record available at https://lccn.loc.gov/2021026227

Contents

CHAPTER ONE — The Specter in the Stacks — 1

CHAPTER TWO — Wrongfully Accused — 26

CHAPTER THREE — The Secret Diary — 43

CHAPTER FOUR — The Language of the Dead — 63

CHAPTER FIVE — The Blue Lady's Revenge — 81

CHAPTER SIX — A Trap Is Set — 99

CHAPTER SEVEN — On Shaky Ground — 112

CHAPTER EIGHT — Biblioghost — 125

CHAPTER NINE — Late-Night Visitors — 138

CHAPTER TEN — The Missing Boyfriend — 157

CHAPTER ELEVEN — The Podcaster's Lair — 173

CHAPTER TWELVE — The Ghost Unmasked — 196

Dear Diary,

PEOPLE REALLY UNDERESTIMATE MY boyfriend, Ned. Between schoolwork and interning at my dad's law practice, Ned can't always tag along on a case or an adventure with my friends. George calls him boring, but I'm proud to be Ned's girlfriend.

How's this for exciting, though? Tomorrow Ned's taking me to a haunted library! Or actually, I'll be taking him, since I'm driving. In his free time, Ned has gotten really into true-crime podcasts, and a few months ago he started producing his own show. He named it *NED Talks*. (I know.)

Ned heard this story about the library's former (and possibly current) resident, a twentieth-century heiress named Harriet Coffin. Apparently, she disappeared one day without a trace, taking the family fortune with her. Ned says her spirit, called the Blue Lady, has been spotted haunting the tower room of her former home. He's determined to find out what really happened to Harriet Coffin and tell the story in one of his podcasts.

I don't believe in ghosts, but I do believe Ned should have someone sensible by his side as he researches the story. After all, I do love a good mystery.

CHAPTER ONE

The Specter in the Stacks

"TURN RIGHT HERE, NANCE! THAT'S THE driveway," said Ned, pointing and bouncing like a kid on his way to the zoo. I think it's cute when he nerds out about a bit of historical trivia or one of my dad's cases, and I was excited to work with him on his investigation.

I put on my turn signal, even though there wasn't a single car in sight, and my car rolled through the imposing iron gate onto a long gravel drive lined with two rows of overgrown cypress trees.

Ned went into tour-guide mode. "The guy who

owned this place was a ruthless water baron. The farmers and the townspeople hated him. He made most of his money by charging such high prices for water that family farmers were eventually forced to sell their land to him at a steep discount."

"Is that Coffin Hall?" I asked, looking at the ivy-covered brick building ahead of us. It looked more like a witch's cottage than a haunted library.

"No, that's the guardhouse. The Coffins made a lot of enemies back in the day."

The driveway snaked past the guardhouse and along the iron fence that marked the edge of the property, up and around a large grassy hill. As we drove, I caught glimpses of a many-roofed mansion at the top. With its trees and mossy statues, the Coffin estate could almost be a park. Except the grass had grown long, and there were no picnickers, no gardeners, no couples strolling, no bird-watchers—not even birds. The estate was completely deserted.

"This place is huge," Ned continued. "The land belongs to the city now. It's a public park. The library's public too, but almost nobody knows about it because it's so far from the center of town."

"Well, who wouldn't want to hang out on the grounds of a haunted library?"

"I know, right? It's the ideal date spot," Ned said, and laughed. "Anyway, after Hieronymous Coffin died, he left his entire estate to his daughter, Harriet. Then she disappeared, leaving behind a cryptic will that said she wanted Coffin Hall to be converted into a library for rare books. Now it has the largest archive of historical documents in the whole state."

"In other words, heaven for a bookworm like Ned," I interrupted. "I'm having trouble getting past the last name Coffin. It just seems too spooky to be real. But I'm also hungry. Did you pack sandwiches?"

"Turkey and cheese. Hieronymous was not a nice guy. But he must have been proud of himself, because he named his daughter Hieronymous Junior."

I furrowed my brow. "I thought her name was Harriet."

"That was the name she went by," Ned explained.

"Would you want to be called Hieronymous Coffin Junior?"

"Harriet Coffin *is* better," I agreed. "Not a bad name for a sleuth, actually."

"I wonder what happened to her. Before she became a ghost, I mean."

"Nobody knows?"

Ned shrugged. "In 1925, a few days after she turned thirty and came into her full inheritance, she just disappeared. She didn't leave a note. All her belongings were still in the house, and there was no sign that she'd packed or made travel plans. Her relatives, her father's lawyer, his business partners—none of them heard anything. Harriet had vanished, and so had the fortune she'd just inherited."

"How did you learn all this? Wikipedia?"

"There's not much about the Coffins online, and Coffin Hall has a pretty basic website. I actually heard the story on a podcast."

"No offense, Ned, but podcasts aren't always reliable historical sources."

"That's exactly why we're going to Coffin Hall: to dig up some primary sources for my own podcast. Look, that must be the Coffin family cemetery!" Ned pointed.

I stopped the car and looked over at the cluster of graves arranged around a three-tiered fountain made of white marble. The basin was dry, and the cemetery was surrounded by a tall chain-link fence. I noticed something yellow moving on the other side of the fence. It looked like there was some kind of excavation going on, complete with dump trucks and an earthmover.

Ned punched my arm lightly. "Eyes on the road, Drew."

"You sound *just* like my dad. We're not even moving!" I pretended to be disgusted but couldn't contain my giggles. Then I put my foot on the accelerator and we made the final ascent to the hilltop.

As the mansion came into view, I almost stopped the car again. There are a lot of grand old buildings in River Heights and the surrounding areas, but Coffin Hall might take the cake. Actually, it kind of looked like a cake. The two-story mansion was built of patterned pink and white brick that accentuated the rows of tall, narrow windows and the roofline, complete with a tower that looked straight out of a storybook castle. Ned had described the architecture as "Victorian Gothic," which made me think of vampires wearing frilly shirts.

In the lot adjacent to the mansion, I parked next to a golf cart decorated with a crow perched inside an ornate letter *C*. "For Coffin," I said, grinning. Ned grabbed his messenger bag from the back seat before climbing out, and we stood in the parking lot for a minute, taking it all in.

"I'm going up to the tower room first," Ned said. "That was Harriet's study. The librarians and patrons say she still haunts it. . . ."

I stared him down. "You can't scare me, Ned Nickerson. Ghosts aren't real. Whatever those people saw was a product of their overactive imaginations. What do you expect to find that will explain Harriet's disappearance?"

"The podcast mentions Harriet's diary. It's written in some kind of code. I think I can crack it."

"A code! Okay, now I'm really interested. But Ned, there has to be a reason no one has cracked it after almost a century."

"I'm going to be the exception. I'm Ned Nickerson, super researcher! That's what *NED Talks* is all about."

"All right, don't get too full of yourself yet. Let's go inside and see what stories the Coffins have to offer. Unless you're chicken?"

"No way. First one inside is a rotten egg!"

Ned and I took off running up the stone steps to the library's front door. We were both out of breath by the time we got to the top. While I waited for my pulse to slow down, I looked around and spotted two stone crows perched over the doorway, looking down at us. There was a crow carved on the front door, too, just above a sign that read COFFIN HALL LIBRARY—A PUBLIC RESOURCE.

Ned took my arm before I could go inside. "We'll have to keep our voices down in there, so let's go over the plan now. I'm going up to the tower room to look through Harriet's papers. Meanwhile, maybe you can ask around about Coffin Hall's history. See if any of the library staff would agree to an interview. I just need a couple of good sound bites. Ghost sightings, levitating books, eerie music, that kind of stuff."

"You want me to encourage people to make up scary stories? That's not my kind of thing, Ned, you know that. . . ."

"No! *NED Talks* isn't a horror podcast. I want to tell the real story of Harriet Coffin. We'll just use the spooky hook to get people interested."

"Okay, as long as we're on the same page here," I said, watching him closely.

"Ha! Good pun," Ned said, pointing to the library sign with a grin.

The library lobby, the mansion's former entryway, was a round, high-ceilinged room with a skylight above a marble-topped circulation desk, where a silver-haired librarian sat in front of a computer. The walls were lined with glass cases displaying old maps and documents, and I spotted another stone crow perched on the archway that led to the main reading room.

The quiet in the building was stifling, interrupted only by the occasional beep of the book scanner and the snuffling of a bored-looking security guard at the entrance to the reading room.

Ned and I approached the circulation desk. I said hello to the librarian, but she didn't look up. She was tiny, no more than five feet tall, but with her strong nose, serious brown eyes, and silver hair swept up in a perfectly smooth chignon, she gave off the unmistakable air of being in charge. A nameplate on the desk read IRENE WISEAU, LIBRARIAN.

"Ms. Wiseau? My name is Nancy Drew, and I'm a resident of River Heights. How do my boyfriend and I sign up for library cards?"

"You may call me Miss Irene," the librarian said primly. I could tell she was the kind of woman who always spoke in complete sentences, who crossed every *t* and dotted every *i* precisely. Miss Irene removed two forms from a file in her desk drawer and slid them across the desk. I wrote in my full name, date of birth, address, and phone number, and Ned did the same. Usually, I would think twice before giving a strange woman my personal details, but I was pretty sure that if anyone could be trusted to keep sensitive information safe, it was a librarian. While I wrote, I tried to get the librarian to come out of her shell.

"My boyfriend, Ned, and I are researching the history of Coffin Hall for his podcast," I said, keeping my voice friendly and open. I decided not to mention the ghost right away.

"The real story of Coffin Hall is written in Harriet's papers, if you have the wherewithal to actually read them. I'm just here to preserve the collection," Miss Irene answered, her face stony.

"But surely you know a lot about the Coffins," I prodded her.

Miss Irene wouldn't budge. "Coffin Hall is a public institution," she said primly. "Its collection belongs to the people. Harriet Coffin willed the house and everything in it to the city. You can read all about it on the library website."

"Yes, we did read that, thank you," Ned replied. "But the episode is actually about Harriet: specifically, what happened to her and the Coffin family fortune. We were hoping to interview someone who knows her story. On the record."

"I don't indulge in speculation or sensationalism when it comes to Harriet Coffin. As I've said, the history of the Coffin family is all public record. All I can do is show you to the relevant documents."

"In my experience, the truth isn't always written down," I said, watching her face carefully. "And people usually know more than they let on."

I noticed a lanyard decorated with enamel pins in the shapes of different birds looped around Miss Irene's neck.

"Cool pins. Is that one a crow?" I asked.

The librarian seemed to warm up a little. "A raven. They're very bright. I keep one as a pet. I find his intelligence refreshing."

"I didn't know ravens were so smart," Ned said.

"Birds are smarter than we think," I replied, and the librarian nodded.

"Corvids like ravens and crows keep stashes of food in many different places," she said. "Science has shown that they can remember up to two hundred locations—what's buried in them, and how quickly the food is decaying."

"They sound smarter than a lot of humans I know," I said.

The librarian's lips twitched slightly in something like a smile. She took the forms from us, looked them over, and then filed each carefully away in the file cabinet behind her. Then she took two cream-colored cards from another drawer and wrote each of our names in blocky capital letters, followed by the date, and handed them to us. The front of each card was printed with a line drawing of Coffin Hall and the letters CHPL.

"Thank you for your help, Miss Irene!" I said, and she nodded.

"I help those who help themselves," she replied.

The librarian turned her back to us, picked up her desk phone, and dialed a three-digit number. "Rosie? Are you in the tower? Come down and cover me, won't you? I'm showing some patrons to the tower room and then I'll be taking my much-deserved break. Please don't dawdle."

Miss Irene hung up the phone. She waited patiently while we passed through the metal detector, underwent a bag check, and signed our names in a register before we could go into the stacks, which seemed like a lot of security for a public library.

The guard who scanned us seemed really checked out, like his mind was somewhere else. He was a handsome, stocky Asian man in his late twenties, with a topknot and beefy forearms.

"Hi!" I said, and he looked up, startled. "I'm doing some research on the history of Coffin Hall for my boyfriend's podcast. Would you like to talk to me on record about Coffin Hall? It would only take a few minutes."

"I'm new here, kid," he said in a bored voice. "And

I'm working a double shift, so I'm not really in the mood to chat."

"Do you mind my asking why you're working double shifts? Can't the library afford other guards?"

"Just the two of us, and the regular guy went on vacation. There's not usually supposed to be a guard here during the day, but after yesterday's incident, Miss Irene called me in. At least the other guy's coming back tonight so I'll finally get a break," Victor answered wearily.

"What happened yesterday?"

"Victor," Miss Irene chided. "No chatting!"

"Sorry, boss," the guard grumbled.

"You can't be distracted and do this job."

"The kid was asking me questions. You want me to be rude? I'm not even supposed to be working right now, man," he grumbled. I heard him and tried to give a sympathetic smile.

I knew better than to interrogate Miss Irene about the incident. Maybe I could get Victor to say more when his boss wasn't breathing down his neck.

Ned and I followed Miss Irene across the empty reading room, which was full of long wooden tables topped by rows of brass reading lamps, and went down a hallway lined with plush carpets and oil paintings of peaceful farms and orchards. The hall ended at a spiral staircase, at the base of which hung a large oil portrait that depicted a young woman with a serious expression, dressed in a light-blue evening dress with a 1920s-style dropped waist and a tasseled skirt made of long strings of silver beads. The portrait sitter wore an elegant silver tiara in her dark hair, and diamonds sparkled on her neck and ears, but the beauty of her attire couldn't hide the sadness in her eyes.

"The Blue Lady herself," Miss Irene said. "Her father had this portrait commissioned to try to entice a husband for Harriet, but she rejected every suitor. This is the way to her tower. From here on, I'll have to escort you."

"Nancy, are you coming with?" Ned asked.

"I'd like some fresh air. Is it all right if I take a stroll through the grounds?"

"Certainly. It's public property. But a word of warning: watch where you step."

I glanced at Victor to see if he'd noticed the librarian's ominous tone, but he had his earbuds in and was humming to himself. Some security guard.

"Let's meet back in the lobby in an hour for an update," I said. "Promise me you'll try not to anger any spirits, living or dead."

"I'll do my best," Ned laughed.

I watched him climb the stairs and disappear into the darkness, feeling uneasy without quite knowing why.

I wandered from room to room without seeing anyone. What was the point of a public library without patrons? Who was I supposed to interview? The librarian and the security guard weren't exactly open books, and I hadn't signed on for ghost hunting. Maybe the grounds would be livelier. . . .

Outside, the sun was high in the sky and the Coffin Hall estate appeared serene, but up close, the lack of upkeep was more obvious. The ground was muddy and the grass was patchy. I had to hop from one spot to the next to keep from getting stuck. Soon I came to the chain-link fence that surrounded the Coffin family graveyard. I'm not a morbid person, but the dry fountain gave me the chills. A plaque at its base read:

DEVOTED DAUGHTER

H. Z. "HARRIET" COFFIN JR.

1895–19XX

LET HER FIND REST

I stared hard at the two *X*s and couldn't help but imagine how I'd feel if I disappeared and no one ever found out what happened to me.

The sound of heavy machinery startled me. On the other side of the cemetery fence, the earthmover had shuddered to life. Construction workers shouted directions over the beeping of trucks. I walked up to the fence and looked out over a huge rectangular hole.

Not far from where I stood, a tall blond woman in

a sharp white suit, snakeskin ankle boots, and a long golden braid was hissing into a walkie-talkie, her back to me.

"I don't want to hear excuses, Jeffrey! I won't apologize for being hands-on. It's my vision. Don't you believe in that? Good! Because it's your job to execute it, so stop wasting time talking to me and get to work!" The woman switched off her walkie-talkie and threw it to the ground. "I'm working so *hard*. I deserve a new purse. *Two* new purses. And a tennis bracelet. I could be in the Cayman Islands right now. Instead I'm here in this hole, up to my waist in mud."

"Excuse me, I couldn't help overhearing—"

The woman's head shot up, and she took me in. She obviously didn't like what she saw. Putting her hands on her hips, she stared down her nose, her perfect red lip curling. "Can I help you? This is private property."

"Where I'm standing is public property."

"Why are you watching me? Are you some kind of cub reporter?"

"I didn't mean to startle you, I'm just a naturally

curious person. My name is Nancy Drew. I'm helping my boyfriend research his podcast. It's called *NED Talks*, because his name is Ned, and he talks. . . . Maybe you've heard of it?"

"I definitely have not. Do I look like someone who listens to podcasts?"

"You don't, you're right. You look like a . . . boss."

"A girlboss, you mean. I always dress for the role," she answered, tossing her braid over one shoulder.

"We're making an episode about the history of Coffin Hall. You must know something about that, seeing as you're excavating right next to it. Would you like to speak on the record?"

"Yes, actually," she answered quickly. "I have a *lot* to say about that eyesore."

"Thanks. I'll start my recorder. Do you mind introducing yourself?" I asked, holding my phone up to the fence.

"Certainly. I'm Yvonne Coughlin, *She*-EO of Coughlin Capital."

"Coughlin . . . Coffin . . . ? Any relation?"

Yvonne continued speaking as though she hadn't heard me.

"I have an MBA from Harvard Business School. Last year I was named one of the Top Ten Women in Real Estate under Thirty by the Developers' Association. And now I have turned my talents to creating the greatest investment opportunity River Heights has ever seen."

"Wow."

"Here's my card. Do you have a card? No? Too bad. Do you know what I love about swans?" Ms. Coughlin said, her eyes sparkling.

"Swans? Weren't we just talking about an investment opportunity?"

I examined her business card, which was printed on heavy paper in fine gold ink. Yvonne had spent a lot of money on the printing. The office address was right in the heart of downtown River Heights, in a swanky new building. Coughlin Capital must have been turning a profit.

"Patience, Nelly. It's all connected. As I was saying,

what I love about swans is how serene and beautiful they look on the surface. Meanwhile, underneath, they're paddling like crazy. That same thing is true of all fashionable women."

"I don't really like swans. They're mean. And my name is Nancy, not Nelly."

"See, if you had a business card, I would've remembered that. What I'm trying to tell you is *I'm a swan*—a visionary. I'm building a pond for other swans—a comfortable home for people like me, who know how to make a real impact."

"What kind of people are those?"

"Movers and shakers! App inventors, designers, content creators, influencers, entrepreneurs, celebutantes, modelebrities."

"So, you're building fancy condominiums?"

Ms. Coughlin's face contorted with disgust. "We don't use that word. I can't stand when people shorten it to 'condo.' Ugh! No, this project is called the Coughlin Cooperative. It's all about building a community that is creative, but also luxurious. Think high-end bohemian. Artist studios with indoor Jacuzzis. My real dream to is create an all-inclusive resort, with hot-yoga studios, gelato shops, luxury boutiques, the works!"

"That sounds . . . fancy," I said. "But what did you want to tell me about Coffin Hall?"

"That building is a safety hazard. I wish they'd condemn it before someone gets hurt. It's only a matter of time, with *those* people in charge. The city refuses to sell the estate to someone who can make real use of it . . . someone like me, for example. It's the perfect location for my resort concept."

"What do you know about the building's history?"

"Who cares what happened a hundred years ago? I've spent too much time stuck in the past. Now I want to live for the future. That's what Coughlin Cooperative is all about."

Yvonne's walkie-talkie crackled from where it was still lying on the ground. "Ms. Coughlin!" someone yelled.

Yvonne rolled her eyes, then picked it up and answered. I couldn't make out what the foreman said to her, but whatever it was, Ms. Coughlin did *not* want to hear it. She gave an angry shriek. "I cannot *believe* this. You're all a bunch of clods! Don't do *anything* until I get there."

It looked like our interview was finished. Ms. Coughlin turned and sashayed away along a plywood walkway, as though she'd forgotten I existed.

"Okay, nice talking with you . . . ," I called after her, watching through the fence a minute longer to see if I could figure out what had happened to make her so upset, but my view was blocked by the row of dump trucks.

I carefully made my way back to Coffin Hall, mulling over my interview with Yvonne. Ned and I were due to meet in the lobby in five minutes. As I approached the library, I heard a faint wailing, like a siren or an alarm, that grew louder as I got closer. I smelled smoke, and up ahead, a black cloud billowed from the window of the tower room where Ned was supposed to be doing his research.

I hurried ahead, no longer worried about the mud.

If Ned was in danger—if he'd gotten hurt while I was wandering around—I'd never forgive myself. I took the front stairs three at a time, and just as I was about to fling open the main doors and run inside to rescue my boyfriend from the flames, Ned barreled through the doorway and ran smack into me.

We both tumbled to the ground and Ned's messenger bag went flying. He scrambled after it, as though he hadn't even seen me. "Hey!" I yelled.

"Sorry," he said. His eyes were wide, and he was out of breath.

"You look scared! Is everything okay?"

"She's after me! We have to go, *now!*" Ned said.

"Who's after you? Miss Irene?" I asked. Ned shook his head, then grabbed the bag and raced toward the car. "What's going on, Ned?"

"Small fire. It's out! Not my fault. I'll explain later. Just—come on!"

I hit the remote unlock button. Ned threw open the passenger door, tossed his bag inside, and dove into the front seat.

Still a little stunned, I tried to get up to follow him, but my ankle had twisted under me when I fell and was already swelling up.

"Help!" I called.

Ned came running back up the stairs. He basically threw me over his shoulder and carried me down as fast as he could. Before we reached the car, I heard a man's voice shouting after us—Victor the security guard?—followed by a furious Miss Irene. Her face was smudged with soot and her hair had escaped its tidy twist.

The librarian raised a trembling finger and pointed it straight at Ned. "Stop, vandal!"

CHAPTER TWO

~

Wrongfully Accused

MISS IRENE AND VICTOR REFUSED TO answer my questions right away. Instead, they hustled us into a conference room and locked us in. While the librarian sat on one side of the table, blocking the door, Victor instructed Ned and me where to sit, then let himself out. He said he was going to "guard the door," but I could clearly hear the sound of the phone game he'd been playing earlier. The library worker Miss Irene had called earlier, Rosie, must have been dealing with the aftermath of Ned's "small fire" upstairs.

The librarian sat silently, peering at us as though she could see right into our brains.

"Aren't you going to tell us what Ned's being accused of?" I asked.

"He knows what he did."

"I don't think he does," I countered. "If either of you want to explain what happened, that would be a start. What was all that smoke?"

"There was a fire," Ned answered. "Some books were involved."

"You're using the passive voice, Mr. Nickerson," scolded Miss Irene. "Fires don't set themselves. Especially not in a building full of very flammable objects. Lucky for you, nothing of value was seriously damaged."

"Lucky?" Ned protested. "You should be thanking me. I triggered the alarm! And I saw who really set the fire—" Ned went pink and looked down. "Never mind. You won't believe me."

"Of course I'll believe you," I said. "After all we've been through, you think I wouldn't trust you to be honest with me?"

"It's not that, it's just—"

"I leave you alone in Harriet's inner sanctum for fifteen minutes, and the whole place nearly goes up in flames! How do you explain that? Speak up, Mr. Nickerson." Miss Irene drummed her fingers against the table impatiently.

"I'm telling you, I didn't start that fire. The Blue Lady did," Ned insisted. I'd never seen such a wild look in his eyes.

"Tell us what happened," I encouraged him.

"She was tall, maybe five eleven, six feet. She was wearing old-fashioned clothes—a dress with a beaded skirt, just like the dress in her portrait. Only this dress was, uh, glowing."

"Glowing?"

"Yeah. There was this weird blue light around her. And she didn't walk like a normal person. I think she was floating. I couldn't see her feet under the skirt, just a weird mist."

"Where did she come from?"

"I don't know. She just *appeared*. Next thing I knew,

books started flying off the shelves. There was a puff of smoke, and some of the books caught fire. I pulled the alarm and used my messenger bag and jacket to stop the fire from spreading."

I looked into Ned's eyes. He winced but held my gaze. I believed him, but I didn't believe that what he'd seen was supernatural.

"I'll tell you what I think," Miss Irene said, narrowing her eyes and wagging her finger at us. "I think this is some sort of prank for the internet. You wanted to use the story of Harriet Coffin to get attention for your little podcast. But your prank went too far, and you got caught."

Ned and I exchanged confused glances.

Miss Irene went to the door and opened it a crack. "Victor, will you come in here, please?" she called.

The security guard shuffled in. "Yes, boss?"

"Did you see anyone in the library today apart from Mr. Nickerson and Miss Drew?"

"They were our only visitors today," he replied.

"So you didn't see a very tall woman floating around, wearing a glowing blue gown?"

"Uh . . . no, ma'am," Victor answered, scratching his head.

"Have you ever seen anyone matching that description in your time here?"

"Can't say I have. I would definitely remember something like that."

"Thank you, Victor. Please go and watch the lobby, and if you do see any glowing women, call me immediately." Miss Irene turned her piercing gaze back to Ned, who was sweating. I couldn't blame him. This tiny librarian was intimidating!

"Well then, Mr. Nickerson. I think we both know it would be best for everyone if you'd just confess."

Ned shook his head. "I'm not going to confess to something I didn't do!"

"I don't think you should say anything else until we get a second opinion," I said.

"I'll let you make your call, but this isn't over," Miss Irene said with a sniff. Then she rose and left the room. The door closed with a click, followed by the *thunk* of a dead bolt.

Miss Irene had locked us in.

When I need advice, there's only one person I call: my father, Carson Drew. He picked up on the first ring.

"Dad, Ned and I are being detained at Coffin Hall. The librarian claims that Ned started a fire in the tower room, but he says he saw someone else do it. Can you come down here right away?"

"Of course. Tell Ned to keep his chin up. I'll be there as soon as I can."

Just as the call ended, someone knocked. It didn't sound like Victor's meaty paw, or Miss Irene's sharp little fist. And my father couldn't possibly be here already.

I put my head against the door to listen. "Who's there?"

"A friend!" a woman's voice replied. "I'm Rosie Gomez, a library volunteer. I'm *the* library volunteer. Miss Irene thinks she runs this place, but she couldn't make it one day without me."

"Nice to meet you, Rosie. I'm Nancy, and I'm in

here with my boyfriend, Ned Nickerson. He's been falsely accused. That's why we're locked in here."

"That's terrible! I don't like talking through this door. If you promise not to run out, I'll open it."

Ned and I exchanged a glance.

"Why would we run away?" I asked. "Our names, phone numbers, and addresses are in your library patron system. And, more importantly, we're innocent."

"I believe you," Rosie replied. "Hang on." I heard the scraping of a key in the lock. "My boss is really upset. She gets like this sometimes. It comes from a good place. She loves this library so much. Too much, if you ask me. Voilà!"

The door swung open, and I stood face-to-face with Rosie Gomez. She was short and curvy with cat-eye glasses and wore her black hair in a shaggy cut with bangs that framed her kohl-lined brown eyes. Rosie looked to be just a few years older than Ned. I noticed her earrings were little silver daggers, each with a dangling red jewel, like a drop of blood, and her black T-shirt had a screen-printed graphic of a bat with its wings outstretched.

Despite her goth style, Rosie's round face was friendly and open. She smiled broadly at us and held out a basket of shiny red apples, individually wrapped cheese and crackers, and two bottles of water. Ned took the basket gratefully while Rosie flopped down in Miss Irene's chair.

"Whew! It's good to sit down. I thought you guys might be hungry or thirsty, and we had some snacks left over from the last Historical Story Time. Actually, we had all the snacks left over. Nobody came. Nobody ever comes. Kids just don't get excited about old surveyors' maps or water-table reports. But that's all right. More for us, right?"

"Now that you mention it, I'm starving," said Ned, tearing into two cheese-and-cracker packages. "Thanks for these. I guess seeing a ghost really works up the appetite."

"We brought sandwiches, remember?" I said.

Ned ignored me and kept happily munching away.

Rosie's eyebrows shot up. "Wait a second, you saw the Blue Lady?"

"I saw someone in the tower room just before the fire. Whoever she was, I'm pretty sure she started it," Ned said before taking a big swig of water.

Rosie groaned. "Oh no, not again."

"This has happened before?" I asked.

"The Blue Lady causing mischief? Yes. But starting fires—that's new."

I frowned. "You really believe the Blue Lady is Harriet Coffin's spirit returning to her home nearly a hundred years after she disappeared?"

"She was the last person to live in this house, and she left it with unfinished business. That's a good recipe for a haunting. But I don't know. . . . I just can't believe that the spirit you saw was Harriet," Rosie said, turning to Ned.

"Why do you say that?" Ned asked.

"The Blue Lady used to be harmless. Sort of helpful, even. Sometimes I'd spend all day looking for a book, and then it'd appear on a shelf I'd already checked twice. Or I'd find all my files rearranged alphabetically. Some mornings I could hear her whistling in the tower. She was nice. I wasn't the least bit afraid of her."

"But now you are?" I asked.

Rosie covered her mouth with her hands before whispering, "Yes."

"When did she change?" asked Ned.

"A little over a year ago. The first incident was right around Valentine's Day. We discovered red ink spilled in our antique map collection. Horrible." Rosie shuddered. "Then strange things started to happen more and more often."

"Like what?" I pressed.

"We found puddles all over the lobby floor and on the tower stairs one morning. Another time, all the portraits of Hieronymous Coffin and his ancestors had been taken down off the walls. Miss Irene dismissed the incidents at first. She only got serious about figuring out who was causing the trouble when books started going missing."

"The *ghost* is stealing books?" I asked. "Anything in particular?"

"Well, someone's stealing them. And so far, what they've taken is pretty boring. It's mostly volumes of regional interest. It happened again yesterday—someone cleaned out a shelf of Coffin family genealogies and left water all over the shelves. Yesterday we had zero visitors, so the only people who could've done it either work here . . . or they never left."

"So you think the Blue Lady is responsible?"

"I don't believe the Blue Lady would ever harm a book. Like I said, she always tried to help me find what I was looking for. That's how I know the Blue Lady really was Harriet Coffin. She cares about what happens in her home."

"Why do you think Miss Irene dragged her feet about the break-ins?" I asked. "She told me it's her responsibility to protect the collection."

Rosie sighed. "She's afraid that Coffin Hall will shut down. When I brought up security cameras, she told me we didn't have the money. Somehow, the board found the money for round-the-clock security guards, though."

"No offense, but your security guard was playing games on his phone all morning," said Ned.

Rosie shrugged. "Victor's okay. I like him a lot better than the older guard, Terry. He thinks he's some kind of big-time ghost hunter."

My phone rang, making us all jump.

"Dad?"

"I'm here. Just parked. How do I find you?"

"There's a security guard named Victor in the main lobby. He can bring you to us."

"Don't worry. I'll be there in a minute. We'll sort this all out. I'm sure it's just a misunderstanding."

"Thanks, Dad. Love you."

As I hung up, Rosie stood to leave. "I'd better go before Miss Irene comes back. And I should take the rest of the snacks with me. Don't need her knowing I was fraternizing with the 'enemy.'"

"It was nice to meet you, Rosie," I said. "I have a feeling this won't be my last visit to Coffin Hall. My friends and I will do our best to figure out who is causing mayhem in the library."

"I hope you do," Rosie replied. "To be honest, I just want our old Harriet back. I miss her whistling. Nobody I know can whistle like that. Must be an old-timey thing. Anyway, good luck, you two."

We waved goodbye and Rosie locked us in again. Two minutes later, I heard my dad's voice and the sound of the door being unlocked again before Victor escorted him inside. "Please wait here, Mr. Drew. I'll get the librarian."

"That won't be necessary. We'll go to her."

We followed Victor out of the conference room to the end of the hallway. When we came to the last door on the right, he knocked and announced, "Boss, Carson Drew is here. He wants to speak with you."

Miss Irene replied, "Enter."

Miss Irene's office was surprisingly cozy. Several comfortable reading chairs were arranged around the room, and two teakwood filing cabinets sat under the curtained window, their contents arranged according to numbers and letters written in a precise hand on small white labels. The only thing out of place was the stack of scorched books piled on one corner of a large antique-looking desk.

Miss Irene sat stock still behind her desk, watching us. My dad settled himself into one of the reading chairs, and Ned and I did the same, though it was impossible to get comfortable under Miss Irene's bright, crowlike stare.

"Well," she said briskly. "I don't have time for sob stories. These children are vandals. They've been sneaking in here, defacing books, stealing. . . ."

"Hang on now. Yesterday was the first time I'd ever heard of Coffin Hall," I objected. "We came here to do research. I told you that when we got here."

My dad, however, was able to remain a lot calmer. "Would you kindly show us your evidence that Ned and Nancy committed arson?"

"These two were our only visitors all day. *This one*"— she jabbed her finger in Ned's direction—"is there in the room when the fire starts, and he says a ghost is responsible. Meanwhile, your daughter is snooping around the grounds doing goodness knows what."

"I'm sorry, Miss Irene, but that argument wouldn't hold up in court. I can vouch for both Ned and Nancy. They're good kids. If you don't have any hard evidence, you'll have to let them go. And on a more personal note, I hope this is the end of the trouble at Coffin Hall. This building is so beautiful. I used to come here back when I was studying for the bar. It was always so quiet."

"Quieter still, these days." Miss Irene sighed. "And the troubles never cease. All right. You may go. But if anything like this happens again, I will report you to the authorities."

We left Miss Irene's office and passed back down the hallway through the reading room and into the main lobby, where Victor was once again lost in his phone game.

Back in the parking lot, Ned heaved a sigh of relief. "I owe you one, Mr. Drew."

"Don't mention it. Do you really believe you saw a ghost?"

Ned blushed. "Well . . . I saw someone who looked like a ghost. She was glowing."

My dad made the *harrumph* sound that means he's considering the evidence and building an argument against it in his head. We Drews have a rational streak that can't be ignored. I knew my dad was adding up all the facts on Ned's side of the equation, and all the facts against it.

"Ned, why don't you ride with me? We have some things to discuss. See you at home, Nancy."

"Okay, fine," I replied, a little frustrated. I had plenty of my own questions for Ned, but they'd have to wait. Ghost or no ghost, there was definitely something weird going on at Coffin Hall. And I was going to get to the bottom of it.

I typed a text to George and Bess before I hit the road. Even though they're my best friends, somehow I didn't want to tell them how big a mess Ned had gotten himself into.

Weird day. Meet at my house in 1 hour? We'll explain there.

They both texted back right away.

Uh, yeah sure, George said.

Are you okay? asked Bess.

Yes, don't worry! See ya soon! I tapped out before hitting send, then started the car, checked my mirrors, and rolled down my windows for some fresh air. In my rearview, Coffin Hall sat huge, silent, and ominous. The window of the tower room was open. The sound of a high, clear melody drifted down, so I leaned out my window to hear better. Someone was whistling from way up high. Whoever they were, they were talented. I didn't recognize the song, but as it seemed to reach a crescendo, the whistler fell silent. I turned off the car and listened for a few more minutes, but didn't hear anything more than the construction equipment next door.

CHAPTER THREE

~

The Secret Diary

WHEN I GOT HOME, I GRABBED MY JACKET from the back seat and remembered that Ned had thrown his messenger bag into my car before Victor hauled him away. When I shouldered it, I realized the bag was heavy—heavier than the notebook, laptop, pencil case, and sandwiches that Ned had brought with him. I'm not in the habit of snooping on my boyfriend, but this time, my curiosity got the better of me. Inside his bag, I found an oversize hardcover volume bound in worn red leather and tied shut with a red leather string. The back cover had scorch marks along two edges. The ornate spine was embossed with the letters *HZC*. Under that was a laminated label with the book's Dewey decimal number.

I tried to review the situation with a cool head. Ned had taken this book from Coffin Hall, but he definitely hadn't checked it out. Which meant he'd stolen it. Why would Ned steal a book he could borrow? Ned had never stolen anything in his life. Once, he found a wallet in the park with cash inside; instead of pocketing the money, he ran—literally ran!—to the owner's home to return it.

Finding the book in Ned's bag didn't necessarily mean he'd done something wrong. Maybe Ned had meant to check it out, but forgot in all the chaos. I guess someone could have planted the book in his bag, but I couldn't think who would want to frame sweet Ned or why.

I tried untying the cord to see inside the book, but the knot was too tight. I was interrupted by two voices calling my name. George and Bess arrived together with a hurricane of questions and wild theories.

"What's going on, Drew?" George asked. "That was some cryptic text you sent."

"Yeah, tell us what's up! I'm dying to know," Bess added.

I paused, trying to think how best to explain the pickle we were in. "Well . . . Ned had an incident at Coffin Hall."

"What kind of incident?" George's smile had vanished.

"There was a fire. I'm not exactly sure what happened."

"Yikes!" said Bess. "Was anyone hurt?"

"Only a few books. The librarian accused Ned of vandalism, which I thought was ridiculous," I replied. "But that was before I found this in his bag." I held up the scorched volume.

"Oh!" Bess cried. "What kind of a person would do that? Book burning is awful! So sixteenth century!" Recently, Bess had taken to carrying poetry books with her everywhere and reading her favorite lines out loud to us.

"Wait," George said. "Why would the library let Ned take a damaged book away with him if they thought he started the fire?"

"Don't you see? Ned snuck it out of the library," I explained. "And then he made me his accomplice by hiding the book in my car so I would take it off the premises."

"No way." George shook her head. "Not our Ned!"

"You're right, I shouldn't jump to conclusions. I'm sure Ned will explain," I said, but I couldn't help feeling worried all the same, and my friends noticed.

"Nancy, stop yanking on that string," Bess ordered. "We don't need to add damaging library property to our list of problems."

"I can't get it untied, and I just want to know what's written inside. The letters on the spine are *HZC*, like Hieronymous and Harriet Coffin. It can't be a coincidence."

"Who?" said George.

"Harriet Coffin is a missing heiress. Her father built Coffin Hall. A volunteer told me her spirit haunts the library now. They call her the Blue Lady."

"Give me the book. I'll open it," Bess said, waggling her fingers. "Long nails come in handy sometimes."

Once I handed it over, Bess gave the book's case a thorough inspection. "Whatever the reason Ned took this, you have to bring it back to Coffin Hall. It could be an important historical document. One of a kind. And it's damaged. The librarians are probably worried sick. They'll need to, like, call a book doctor."

"You're right. Of course we'll take it back. I just want to hear Ned's side of the story first. The full story. He told the librarian he saw someone in the room with him just before the fire—a woman—but Ned and I were the only visitors all day. Ned said this woman was dressed in old-fashioned clothes. And she was, uh, *glowing*. Like she wasn't of this world. Like—"

George burst out laughing. "Let me get this straight. Ned said a ghost started the fire? Those true-crime podcasts have really gone to his head!"

"He didn't exactly say it was a ghost. He said it

was a woman whose clothes gave off a blue light. But he seemed sincere. Honestly, I don't even think Ned knows how to lie."

"He's not a golden retriever, Nancy," George replied. "He might lie if he has a good reason."

I sighed. "Even if he was exaggerating for the librarian, I don't think he'd lie to me if I asked him directly. He's probably in Dad's office explaining the whole thing right now."

Bess, George, and I went inside and sat down in the dining room. Only then did I realize how hungry I was. My mind had been racing so fast I'd forgotten to eat the sandwiches Ned had packed. Hannah read my mind and brought out some hummus and pita bread with vegetables to snack on.

"Thanks, Hannah, you're a lifesaver," I said, crunching down on a carrot stick.

"Returned from the land of the dead, have you?" she said. "I heard you went to Coffin Hall today. Did you see the ghost?"

"As a matter of fact—"

"Nancy, I untied the knot!" Bess exclaimed, holding the book open.

I dropped my carrot and leaned in. The pages were covered with cursive handwriting in pencil, tiny, neat letters crammed into countless rows that were divided into three columns. I had to squint to read the faded writing. Even with my nose practically touching the page, I still couldn't make heads or tails of it. The letters were unfamiliar, more like symbols than an alphabet, and I couldn't follow the logic of the page. Were these sentences or mathematical equations, and how did one column relate to the next?

Once George got her eyes on the page, she could barely stay in her seat. "What is this? Secret code?"

"Maybe . . ." I flipped to the front of the book, where there was an inscription written in ink in the same hand, and, more importantly, in English: *The Diary of Harriet Z. Coffin. 1918–1925.*

Under the inscription was a stamp in red ink: *Property of the Coffin Hall Rare Books Collection. Not to be removed from the premises.*

"Oh my gosh," said George. "Did Old Man Nickerson steal a ghost's diary?"

A book like this was probably kept in a special case, and maybe even locked up. How had Ned gotten a hold of it without Miss Irene's help, and why on earth didn't he put it back where it belonged?

"That's it. I'm not going to wait another minute," I said, standing up from the table. "I'm going to find out why this book ended up in Ned's bag."

I burst into my dad's office without knocking. Bess and George were hot on my heels.

"Girls," Dad said in a cautionary tone.

"Sorry to barge in." I turned to Ned, holding out Harriet's diary. "I found this in your bag, and I don't think Miss Irene knows it's missing. Can you please tell me what you're doing with it? How did you even get your hands on Harriet's actual diary in the first place?"

"The case was unlocked. I thought Miss Irene had left it open for me before she took her break so she wouldn't have to come back upstairs," Ned explained.

"Hello, did we meet the same librarian? Because I didn't get the sense that Miss Irene would be thrilled to let us paw through Harriet's diary unsupervised."

Ned dropped his head into his hands and groaned. "Yeah, you're right, it doesn't make any sense. But I couldn't do much pawing, anyway. I couldn't even get the darn string untied! When the alarm went off, I panicked. The room was filled with smoke, so I just grabbed everything on the table and got out of there as fast as I could."

"So you knew you had the diary the whole time we were being interrogated by Miss Irene? Why didn't you come clean?"

"You heard Miss Irene. She'd never believe that I accidentally stole the diary, and she probably would've called the police. So I kept my mouth shut."

"Ned, this isn't just any old book," I told him as kindly as possible. "It's one of the library's prize possessions. You have to return it. It won't be long before Miss Irene notices it's missing."

Ned nodded. "I know. I will, and I'm sorry. But first, I really want to look inside."

He took the book and laid it open on my dad's desk. The five of us crowded around, scanning the tables of cryptic symbols.

"I heard about Harriet's diary on a ghost podcast," Ned told us. "No one has ever cracked her code, so no one knows what it says. Maybe I'm foolish for thinking this, but when I heard about her, I was sure I could find out what happened to her. Finding her missing family fortune would be a sweet bonus. Fortunately, I know this really smart girl with a lot of experience in solving mysteries. . . ."

"Secret codes are so romantic." Bess sighed dreamily. "I'd love for someone to write me a letter in code. A love letter, but our secret love is forbidden, and there are spies everywhere, trying to tear us apart—"

"These symbols do look a little familiar," said George, elbowing her cousin in the side. "Look, this one repeats the most, so . . . that must be *E*."

George and Bess started coming up with possible translations. I noticed something sticking out between the last page and the back cover. Gently grabbing the edge, I drew out an old photograph in a black card-board frame—a portrait of a frowning young woman with large, transfixing eyes, her hair pinned up around her head like a cloud. She was posed beside a small table, one hand resting on an open book.

Ned gasped when he saw the picture. "That's her! That's the woman I saw in the tower room. Same hair, same outfit."

"You said she was very tall, right?" I asked. "I guess it's hard to tell from this photo. . . ."

"Whoa! Don't you think she looks a little like Bess?" George exclaimed.

Bess wrinkled her nose. "I can't really picture myself wearing something so . . . distinguished."

Ned grabbed my arm and held my gaze. "I really think I saw Harriet's ghost. But Nancy . . . maybe she's the one who unlocked the case. I think she wanted me to take the diary."

"Now, how could you know that?" asked my dad. He'd been uncharacteristically silent the past few minutes, but I could tell he was listening carefully.

"Just a feeling. I think Harriet knew there was going to be a fire, and she thought I would keep it safe."

Dad sighed. "I wish it were that easy to communicate with the dead. Really, I do. But it's impossible. And legally speaking, it's irrelevant. No matter what you think a dead woman may or may not have wanted, you still took something that wasn't yours."

"What is happening to me?" Ned cried.

"In my experience, the simplest answer is usually the right one. And right now, 'a ghost did it' is not a simple answer," said Dad.

"Right now, you're the most obvious suspect," I added.

Ned groaned. "I'm getting a stomachache."

"All right, you Drews, there's no need to grill the poor kid," Bess said. "He obviously feels terrible."

"Oh, you're fine, son. Just hungry." Dad shoved away from his desk. "Come with me. We'll get Hannah to make us something more substantial. After we eat, Nancy can drive you back to Coffin Hall so you can return the book and apologize to Miss Irene again. The longer you hold on to it, the guiltier you'll look, understand?"

Ned nodded mutely, and Dad escorted him out of the office, leaving Bess, George, and me with Harriet's diary. I took another look, but the letters had a funny way of crawling out from under my eyes. Turning page after page only revealed more of the same.

"We can totally crack this," George said. "I think it's some kind of substitution cipher. Remember that secret decoder ring I used to have?"

"How could I forget the only piece of jewelry you ever liked?" Bess said. "Or that I was the one who lost it?"

"Right," I added with a small smile. "That was the time we were tracking the smugglers in the storm drain." George had been really upset. She'd loved that ring.

"Anyway, the ring showed you how to swap one letter for another. So, *A* equals *G*, *B* equals *H*, *C* equals *I*, et cetera. We just have to find the key to this code to figure out which letters to swap to decode the message."

"You act like it's so easy," Bess complained. "Don't you think the librarians have already tried to crack this, along with lots of other people way smarter than us?"

"She's right," I said. "This code is not going to be solved with a ring from a cereal box."

George frowned but didn't say anything.

"I do want to know what happened to Harriet," I continued. "And I want to know where the Coffin family fortune went. Maybe that's all written down right here. Still, before we get caught up in secret codes, we have to focus on something more important: clearing Ned's name."

I left my friends to their decoding and returned to the dining room, where Ned and Dad were drinking iced tea, having already demolished half a ham-and-asparagus quiche. Usually, Ned cheers up after he's eaten something, but he still looked miserable. I served myself a slice, then took a seat next to him and put an arm around his shoulders, but he wouldn't look at me.

Taking the hint, Dad rose from the table, muttering something about a conference call.

"Are you okay?" I asked once Ned and I were alone.

"I didn't like hearing you call me a suspect. That hurt. But you're right. My story sounds totally made up."

"I don't think you made it up. You saw someone in that room. I just don't believe it was the ghost of Harriet Coffin."

"Why not? Lots of other people have seen her. Like Rosie."

I still wasn't sure how reliable Rosie's story was, but she did know a lot about Coffin Hall, and she'd been kind to us.

"Let's say the spirit of Harriet Coffin does haunt her former home. Rosie said the Blue Lady used to be friendly, and something's changed recently. Suddenly this spirit who always took care of her home is trying to destroy it. What changed?"

"What are you saying?"

"It's possible this new, nasty version of the Blue Lady isn't Harriet at all. What if it's someone else—someone living—who wants people to think they're seeing a ghost?"

Ned considered my theory while I picked at my slice of quiche. "I guess it wouldn't be the first time you discovered someone pretending to be a ghost. She really looked otherworldly, though."

"What I don't understand is why anyone would spend so much time in that run-down old building. I mean, anyone besides you, Ned."

"Hey!"

"You saw it yourself. The place was deserted. They don't have any fun reads or cool picture books for kids. Just row after row of books and historical documents. Nope, the only people who still want to spend time in Coffin Hall are history nerds and academic researchers."

"I'd argue that history is valuable," Ned countered. "If you lose the firsthand account of an event, it's easy to forget what really happened. Then someone else can swoop in and sell you a new story."

"Most petty criminals aren't in the business of

rewriting history. They just want money or goods they can sell."

"Or revenge. Maybe someone has a grudge against Miss Irene. We know she isn't easy to get along with. It could be a disgruntled ex-librarian. Someone she fired."

"Come on. Help me clear the table, and then grab your jacket and Harriet's diary. We're going back to Coffin Hall."

Ned grimaced. "Can't it wait till tomorrow? I've had enough of that place for one day. I'm the last person Miss Irene wants to see right now. And what if the ghost does something else while we're there, and I get blamed for it? I'll be locked up for sure."

"I'm sorry, Ned, but my dad's right. You may not have started this mess, but you do have to help clean it up."

"Fine. But I'll need you to distract Miss Irene and the guard while I go upstairs. I don't want to be caught with the diary, and I don't think Miss Irene would accept 'I'm trying to return it' as an explanation."

"If you want my help to clear your name, you have

to help me clear the table first. And do the dishes, too."

"Fair enough," Ned said, before he balanced two plates on his arms, took a cup in each hand, and walked gingerly to the kitchen. He moved like a clown or a very old man, which made me laugh. There was no way this silly boy would ever harm a book. I had to find the evidence to prove he hadn't set that fire. If the library didn't have the money for a security camera or attentive guards, maybe I could offer my services for free. Lucky for me, I happened to know someone with a large collection of electronics.

Ned caught me as I was about to leave the dining room. "Thanks, Nancy. I mean it."

"Don't mention it," I said with a small smile.

While Ned took care of the dishes, I checked on George and Bess. They were still in my dad's office, deep in discussion about possible translations of a particular section in the middle of the diary. Bess was carefully photographing page after page with the camera on her cell phone.

"Well, did you crack it yet?" I asked, startling Bess.

"Not yet," George replied. "It's a little trickier than I thought it would be."

"Huh, no kidding." I picked up the diary and flipped through it again, noting that the weird scratchy letters were just as illegible as before, then snapped the book shut and tucked it under my arm.

"Hey, I'm not done with that!" Bess protested.

"If we're going to crack this, we'll need digital backups of all the pages," George added.

"George, this is exactly what librarians are for. We have to return the diary to its caretakers. Ned and I are going back to Coffin Hall, and I want you two to come with us."

"Now?" said Bess. "George and I were excited to work on this code!"

"Sorry, guys, but that's not the priority right now. I need to find some evidence that supports Ned's story, and soon. If this so-called ghost strikes again, I want to be prepared. Besides, I don't think it's a good idea for us to hang on to stolen property."

"I guess you're right," George said. "Bess took

enough photos for us to work with. But how do you expect us to help you catch a ghost?"

"I'm glad you asked. George, do you still have your webcam from the animation class you took last summer?"

"That class ruled. I'm making GIFs now. And, yeah, I think I have a few webcams in my closet somewhere."

"Can you go dig those out? And we'll need some tools to install them. I'll pick you up in fifteen minutes."

"I'll grab my dad's toolbox. See you soon!" George put on her jacket, gave us a little wave, and left.

"Nancy, do you really believe Ned's innocent?" Bess asked once the front door closed. "He could have started that fire by accident. Maybe he just panicked and told the ghost story to cover his tracks."

"Ned wouldn't lie to me. He just wouldn't. If believing him means I have to investigate a ghost for arson, then that's what I'll do!"

CHAPTER FOUR

The Language of the Dead

GEORGE, BESS, NED, AND I TOOK THE winding road back to Coffin Hall. Bess put on her favorite boy band at top volume. When we turned onto the long driveway and followed the line of cypress trees toward the library, the sugary lyrics and sunshiny vocals suddenly sounded eerie. Even the normally bubbly Bess was quiet.

Across the chain-link fence, the construction site was silent, the machinery deserted, even though it was only four o'clock in the afternoon. I wondered where Yvonne Coughlin, the hands-on CEO, had gone. I doubted someone like her would want to live so far from the glitz and glamour of the city, so how did she plan to convince people to spend big bucks on a condo in the middle of nowhere next to a crumbling old building everyone said was haunted?

This time, when we pulled into the visitors' lot, we weren't alone—a fire truck and a River Heights police car were parked near the entrance. Ned slumped down in his seat so his face wasn't visible in the window. "I'll wait to go in until the coast is clear."

As I climbed out of the car, someone zoomed past on a longboard. It took me a moment to realize it was Victor, the security guard. His long black hair flew free from its topknot, and he had a big grin plastered on his face.

"Hi, Victor!" I called. "Remember me?"

He jumped off the board and popped it into his hand. "How could I forget? You made a pretty big scene here today. Back so soon? And who are these two?"

I laughed. "That's right, back again. This is Bess and that's George. They're my best friends. We're going to catch the *real* culprit and clear my boyfriend's name."

"Hi," said Bess.

"Sick wheels," George added.

"Thanks." Victor grinned. "I've been using my breaks to practice power sliding." He jumped back on the board and tried to demonstrate, but hit a rock and went flying off.

Bess ran over to help him up, but Victor dusted himself off and shrugged.

"I'm okay. It's about the journey, you know? I'm off the clock now. Tell me about your plan to catch the ghost."

"It's simple," I said. "Cameras."

"You've got special ghost cameras?"

"Just regular web cameras. I'm pretty sure the person breaking into the library is alive. They're just pretending to be a ghost, for some reason."

"Hey, I hope you catch them. I thought this job would be a piece of cake, but boy was I wrong. This place creeps me out, especially at night. I've heard weird sounds coming from under the floor. Sometimes it's running water. Other times, I swear I've heard someone splashing around down there."

Just then the library doors opened and Miss Irene came out with a firefighter. "What an ordeal," she groaned. "Rosie's about to go home for the day, and I still have to take inventory of all the books that were damaged. Victor, can you do a couple more hours of overtime to help me out?"

"Respectfully, no thanks, boss," Victor replied. "I've had enough for today. Isn't Terry going to be here soon? He'll be more help than I am anyway, he's the Coffin Hall expert after all."

Miss Irene sighed dramatically, then noticed us standing off to the side. "Miss Drew," she called, her tone unmistakably chilly. "I'd hoped I'd seen the last of you."

"Hi, Miss Irene. After today, I know you must be exhausted, but my friends and I are here to help. This is George Fayne, and her cousin—" Before I could finish introducing her, Bess interrupted with a high-pitched squeal.

"Miss Irene! Is that you?"

"Elizabeth Marvin! It's been too long. How *are* you?"

To my great surprise, the chilly librarian opened her arms and embraced Bess like a long-lost friend.

"How's Mr. Prettyfeathers? Does he still steal your jewelry?"

"Yes, he's an awful thief," Miss Irene said, laughing.

"Who's Mr. Prettyfeathers?" asked George.

"He's my pet raven," Miss Irene explained. "He had quite a crush on your friend."

"Most males do," said George. "Bess, how do you know this lady's bird?"

"Miss Irene taught the poetry seminar I took at the arts center last summer. She introduced me to Emily Dickinson and the Brontë sisters, and so many other great women writers!"

"Yes, Miss Marvin is quite a promising young poet," Miss Irene said. "I still remember that line you wrote about the sunflowers."

Bess blushed.

"I had no idea you wrote poems!" I said. "Why haven't you shown them to us?"

"I would have if you asked. You and George aren't exactly into that sort of thing."

"That's not true," I protested. "I like riddles!"

"Riddles are *not* poetry," Miss Irene replied with a sniff. "They are logic puzzles."

I grinned. "That's why I like them."

"What about limericks? Those are fun," George said.

Bess gave her cousin an annoyed look. "Limericks are just bad jokes. Poetry is powerful. It moves you. Makes you see the world differently."

"I taught you well, Elizabeth," said Miss Irene, smiling. "Now, may I ask why you associate with these two suspicious characters?"

Bess raised her eyebrows. "Do you mean Ned and Nancy? You don't need to worry about them. Nancy's the best crime solver in River Heights, and Ned is one of the good guys."

Miss Irene rolled her eyes. To say Ned and I had made a bad first impression on her might have been an understatement. How was I going to distract the librarian long enough for Ned to return the diary? Coffin Hall needed better security, but the library didn't have the budget. I decided to offer my services, pro bono.

"Miss Irene, please. I feel terrible about what happened today, and I know Ned didn't set the fire, so I thought maybe I could help you find out who did. Let's go inside and I can tell you more."

With Bess's encouraging hand on her arm, Miss Irene nodded and led us up the stairs. Victor ran up ahead to hold the front door for her. Behind us, I heard the faint click of my car door shutting, but I didn't look over my shoulder, worried I'd give Ned away.

We returned to Miss Irene's office. Bess and George settled into the armchairs facing the desk, but I was too nervous to sit still. As Miss Irene was settled in her chair, I unzipped my backpack, took out George's cameras, and placed them on the desktop.

"We'd like to set up these webcams in the locations

where the ghostly activity seems most common—one in the lobby, one on the stairs to the tower, and one in the room itself."

Miss Irene picked up one of the cameras and eyed the lens suspiciously. "Your generation thinks technology can solve everything. I've had security guards on duty every night, and they haven't been able to put a stop to these incidents."

Was Coffin Hall even wired for internet? The building looked like it was stuck in another time.

"If we can connect these cameras to your Wi-Fi, they'll stream to George's laptop, so we'll be able to see if anyone sneaks in after-hours, and we'll be able to record any evidence to share with the police. It shouldn't take us long to spot the perpetrator." As I spoke, I tried to catch Bess's eye. I needed her to help convince Miss Irene.

Bess gave me a small nod before picking up where I'd left off. "This library is such a special place. We just want to help you protect it."

Miss Irene gave a sad smile and her eyes filled with

tears, but she didn't cry. "This institution weighs on me, girls. I feel responsible for keeping it afloat. But there are fewer patrons every year. The empty rooms, the unloved books, the deserted grounds . . . this is not what Harriet Coffin envisioned when she gave her home as a gift to the people of River Heights to enjoy."

Miss Irene stood and went to the cabinet closest to the door, pulled open one of the drawers, took out a folded piece of paper, and handed it to me.

The paper was thick and yellow, the creases worn deep. I opened it carefully and was surprised to see that the document in my hands was Harriet Coffin's last will and testament. I recognized the handwriting of the signature from her diary. "I feel like I should be wearing gloves or something," I said with a nervous laugh.

"It's only a copy," Miss Irene said. "Don't worry."

I read the first line of the document out loud: "'I, Hieronymous Zenas Coffin II, called Harriet, of River Heights, being of sound mind and body, and considering the uncertainty of this frail and transitory life, do hereby make, ordain, publish, and declare this to be my last will and testament. If you are reading this, you may assume I am dead.'"

"It's a beautiful document," Miss Irene murmured. "Harriet was a bit of a poet. Her father hired all the best private tutors for her, but he wouldn't allow her to leave River Heights or take a paying job. Hieronymous said his daughter was only fit to be the wife of a rich man."

"How did you get interested in Harriet's story, Miss Irene?" Bess asked. Somehow my friend's sweet face and talent for compliments managed to charm even the toughest customers. Miss Irene was no exception.

"When I took this position after completing library school, I intended to stay only a few years, but as I spent more time with Harriet's collection, I stopped thinking about my next move. Harriet wrote several books, mostly local histories, transcriptions of interviews with farmers and other craftspeople, that sort of thing. She cared deeply about life in this town, and she made me care about it too. I've spent over half my life here."

"River Heights is full of surprises," I said, thinking of all the interesting people I'd met and all the mysteries I'd solved right here in my own backyard.

"What does Harriet's will say?" Bess asked.

"Miss Drew, will you kindly give me the will to read the relevant selection?" Miss Irene asked. When I did, Miss Irene pointed to a sentence in the second paragraph.

"'Coffin Hall and its contents shall be donated to the people of River Heights and converted into a public library.' There you have it, in her handwriting."

"She was so generous!" Bess exclaimed.

"Is there anything about the family fortune?" George asked.

"Just one line," Miss Irene said, reading again from the document. "'The Coffin coffers are closed to all Coffins living and Coffins not yet born.'"

"Whoa, cryptic," George mused.

"She really was a poet," said Bess.

"What do you think happened to the money?" I asked Miss Irene point-blank.

She blinked owlishly at me. "The city pays my salary, but everything else is run on donations, and those funds are drying up. Do you know, I used nearly the entire year's budget to hire those security guards and lease that metal detector, and what has it gotten me? I'd offer you tea, girls, but there isn't enough to go around. . . ."

Now Miss Irene was crying, covering her face with her hands. Bess got up and patted her back.

When Miss Irene had calmed down again, George gently asked again, "What happened to the Coffin fortune?"

"No one knows," the librarian said miserably. "The accounts were all cleaned out the day before Harriet went missing. She cashed out every last cent. Some people thought it was Harriet's revenge against her greedy relatives, who tried to force her to leave Coffin Hall after her father's death. Others believed the relatives did away with her to take the fortune for themselves."

"Did away with—Do you mean they think she was murdered?" George's eyes were wide.

"I sincerely hope not," Miss Irene replied, folding her hands.

Now that she seemed to be more open, it felt like the perfect moment to try to get some answers for Ned. "You've spent a lot of time with Harriet's writing. What do you think happened to her?"

Miss Irene gave that same sad smile. "I'm a romantic. I like to believe she found love somewhere. You know, there was a man who courted her when she was young—William Bratt. He was a piano tuner. But Harriet's father forbade them from marrying. William was conscripted into the army and never returned to River Heights. He may have died in the war. . . ."

After a moment, Miss Irene stood again and went to the other filing cabinet. This time she pulled out a stack of letters tied together with ribbon.

"Harriet and William wrote in secret for five years, before he went away to war. Harriet saved every letter he sent her. Everyone who knew Harriet knew she was devoted to him. When the letters were discovered in the tower room two weeks after her disappearance, the caretakers of the Coffin estate were finally convinced that Harriet was dead, and at that time the property passed into public trust. I've kept William's letters in my personal collection, even though I know I should have them out on display. I tell myself no one would be able to read them, so what's the point? I suppose I feel protective of this love that was never to be." Miss Irene untied the ribbon and held out the letters to us.

George, Bess, and I each took an envelope and carefully removed its letter. As I looked at the sheet, it became clear to me why no one would be able to read it: the letters were written in code, and it looked like the same code we'd seen in Harriet's diary.

George yelped, but I pinched her leg and gave her a warning look.

"Oh wow. It's a secret code!" Bess said. "What does it say?" She was doing a much better job of pretending.

Miss Irene sighed. "Another mystery. Harriet's diary is part of our collection, and it's written the same way, but even after years of research, I haven't been able to decode a word, and neither have any volunteers or researchers. I can go get the diary. It's page after page of this—"

"No need!" I said quickly. "We're not here to solve this particular mystery. At least not at the moment. Right, George? We just want to find out who's been breaking into the library, and how."

"I guess," George muttered. "But you have to admit this is pretty cool, Nancy."

"And romantic," Bess chimed in. "Poor Harriet! Poor William! I can see her, locked away in her tower, writing letters in a language only she and her beloved could read. Oh! That gives me a good idea for a poem. . . ."

George chuckled. "She takes one creative writing class and suddenly she's William Shakespeare."

"More like I'm Elizabeth Barrett Browning. Don't get it twisted."

Someone knocked on the office door and we all jumped.

"Who is it?" Miss Irene called.

"It's me, Rosie. I forgot my phone again."

"Come in!"

Rosie opened the door. "Just popping in to say good ni— Oh, Nancy Drew! Not in trouble this time, I hope?"

"No, not this time," I said with a smile. "These are my friends, George and Bess. It's actually thanks to you that we're here. Remember how you wanted to get security cameras, but Miss Irene said the library didn't have the money for it?" I held up the cameras. "Well, here they are! Free of charge."

"Oh, thank you, Nancy! That's fantastic!" Rosie exclaimed. "I know you'll find something to prove these terrible incidents aren't Harriet's fault."

"I think you might be right about that. We were hoping to get the cameras up before dark in case the culprit tries again tonight." I turned back to Miss Irene. "Would that be okay?"

She sighed. "Yes, I suppose. As long as I don't have to do anything technical."

"We'll need the Wi-Fi password," George said.

"Rosie knows all that. She's the tech wizard around here."

"Actually, my partner and I had plans to work on some art together, and I wasn't planning on staying late—"

"Can you find the ladder and show the girls where to put the cameras up? I don't want them to ruin the antique beams. Thanks, Rosie. You're my super volunteer."

"Rosie knows this, Rosie does that," Rosie grumbled, but Miss Irene ignored her.

"Oh, what am I going to tell the library board? If I tell them these ghost incidents have posed a danger to patrons, they'll have my head on a plate! Speaking of which, is anyone hungry? I'll order us some pizza. Maybe that will convince Victor to stick around for a few hours of overtime. . . ."

"I can't believe I put up with this drama for free," Rosie muttered, just loud enough for me to hear. She took a deep breath. "No anchovies this time, Miss Irene. Please, I'm begging you; it stinks up the whole library. All right, Nancy, George, Bess, follow me."

"Leave the letters here, if you don't mind," said Miss Irene.

George blushed crimson, caught in the act of

slipping the envelope into the pocket of her denim jacket. Shamefaced, she slid it across the desk. "Sorry. I was just curious."

"I know the idea of cracking that code is enticing," Miss Irene replied coolly, "but I can't allow the letters to leave my office. I need to keep them safe."

George gathered up her cameras and we followed Rosie out of the office and down the hall into the reading room. The late afternoon sun filtered through the tall stained-glass windows, and colorful shadows stretched out along the aisles of books. Coffin Hall had some charm left, after all. It was too bad more people didn't know about this place. I wouldn't have minded curling up in an armchair with a mystery novel, a mug of tea, and a purring cat.

But abandoned like this, the library was undeniably spooky. Every small sound put me on high alert. It would be hard to relax here knowing a phantom was lurking in some corner, waiting for her next opportunity to strike.

CHAPTER FIVE

The Blue Lady's Revenge

GEORGE BEGAN INSTALLING THE FIRST camera in the lobby. Rosie stood below to steady the ladder. As Bess connected the cameras to Wi-Fi on George's laptop, I started worrying that we might cross paths with Ned as he snuck down from the tower. After ten minutes with no sign of him, my thoughts morphed into worry that something had happened to him.

I sent him a quick text: Status update?

No reply.

We're installing the first cam in the lobby. Stairs next. Then tower. I hoped I'd given Ned enough warning. Miss Irene seemed busy enough shut up in her office, and Bess had turned on the classic Marvin charm to keep Rosie occupied with a conversation about eyeliner techniques.

But then Rosie excused herself to use the restroom. Worried she might run into Ned on her way, I said I had to go too and tailed her through the main reading room and into the hallway, following the signs that pointed toward the water fountains and restrooms. After she went in, I realized I had a few minutes to check on Ned. I sprinted down the hallway in the opposite direction, but before I reached the staircase, my foot hit a slippery patch and my legs went out from under me.

I'd managed not to hit my head, and as far as I could tell, none of my bones were broken. Where had the water come from? I looked for a fire sprinkler or a knocked-over water bottle, but there was no sign of its source. And this wasn't the only wet patch. In fact, the puddles seemed to lead straight to the staircase.

I hauled myself up and carefully tested my ankle, which twinged but could take enough weight to walk on. Still, those stairs would be a challenge.

I was slowly making my way across the floor when I heard a sound that made me stop short: a woman screaming for help. The voice didn't sound like George or Bess. *Miss Irene? Rosie?* I hesitated at the foot of the stairs but didn't hear anything coming from the tower, not even a whistle. Whatever Ned was up to, it could wait. I turned and hobbled as fast as I could toward the restrooms, this time keeping an eye on the floor for wet spots.

Rosie was pushing hard against the women's restroom door as if trying to keep something inside, but after a few seconds, the door burst open, releasing a wave of muddy water all over the library's carpets and marble floors. The men's restroom was flooding too, along with both water fountains. I watched in horror as the streams joined together, rushing down the hall toward the offices and conference rooms, soaking carpets, wallpaper, and the books on the lowest shelves.

"Rosie!"

When she turned, her face was pale. "Miss Irene is going to kill me."

"What happened?" I tried to wade closer to her without getting swept away.

"I don't know! When I went into the bathroom, water started shooting out of the toilets and sinks."

"How do we stop it?"

"Someone will have to go down to the basement and turn off the water. Why did Terry have to pick this week to go on vacation? He's the only one who goes down there."

"Terry's the more experienced security guard, I take it?"

"He's been coming to Coffin Hall since he was a kid. Knows the place inside and out. I'll call him."

Rosie climbed onto a chair to get out of the current, then dialed a number on her cell phone. I watched her face fall.

"Hi, Terry? It's Rosie. I know you're not due in until six, but it's an emergency. Something's wrong with the plumbing. The bathrooms are flooding. . . . Everything's flooding! Can you call me back as soon as you get this? Or better yet, come help. Hurry, please!"

"Where's the basement entrance?" I asked when she hung up. "I'm not sure we can wait for Terry. If we're lucky, we can shut off the water before it reaches Miss Irene's office."

Rosie nodded and led me back into the reading room, stopping to grab a toolbox and a flashlight from a supply closet on the way. We continued past more shelves to a small wooden door labeled NOT AN EMERGENCY EXIT. Rosie extracted a ring of keys from her jacket and selected one, but when she went to insert it in the lock, the door swung open.

"Well, now we know a ghost didn't cause this flood," I said. "A spirit would just pass through the door."

"I guess you're right." Rosie reached for the light switch. I heard a click, but the basement stairs stayed dark.

"The bulb must have burned out. Do you mind

going down first? I'm not great with high-pressure situations. That's why I wanted to work in a library in the first place. I thought this would be a good way to get out of my shell and meet people."

Rosie shone her flashlight down, but the beam wasn't strong enough to reach the bottom.

More stairs. Great. Oh well, I told myself. *I can wrap and ice my ankle the minute I get home.*

"Sure, I don't mind going first," I assured Rosie. "I've been in plenty of spooky basements. No big deal."

I turned on the flashlight app on my phone and began my slow descent, hanging on to the handrail to keep the weight off my still-smarting ankle.

Rosie chattered nervously behind me. "I live with my grandma—help her around the house and stuff—but I get bored if I don't have enough to do, so I started volunteering a couple hours a week here. Then I just got sucked in. Now I come here thirty, sometimes forty hours a week if Miss Irene is really overwhelmed. She used to have a real assistant librarian, but he got laid off last year when the board cut our operations budget."

The basement stairs were old and creaky. It seemed like they hadn't been updated since Harriet herself lived here. But somehow the stairs held, and Rosie and I made it to the bottom in one piece.

I cast my light around the room. The low-ceilinged room was filled with a tangle of copper and silver plumbing running through the walls and ceiling. The air hummed with the sound of water rushing through pipes. A few had sprung leaks, leaving puddles on the floor. I spotted valves at different intersections of pipe, but no sign of where the master controls might be. I got down on my knees and crawled under the pipes to check on the other side of the tangle. When the light from my phone hit the back wall, instead of a control panel or a big red button, I saw the outline of a metal plate painted to match the wall. It was almost invisible, except for hinges on one side and a small latch on the other that seemed to be stuck fast. A door, but where did it lead?

"Rosie!" I called. "What's with this weird door? Why doesn't it open?"

"A door? I don't think so. It's probably just an old control panel or something."

"Huh. Maybe Terry would know. . . ." I tried working my fingers into the crack, but it was no use. The door was shut tight. I crawled out from under the pipes and rejoined Rosie.

"There it is!" she called, pointing her flashlight at a small metal sign that read BACKFLOW PREVENTER. The valve above it was in the off position. She tried turning it with her fingers, but the mechanism was stuck. Rosie took a long-handled wrench from her toolbox and fitted it around the valve, then threw her weight against the wrench. The valve didn't budge.

"Nancy, help me!" she said.

I obliged and wrapped both hands around the wrench. On the count of three, we pushed together as hard as we could. Slowly, the stuck valve gave way and creaked into the on position. The pipes around us began to shake and shudder as the stream of water slowed to a trickle. Once the flow stopped completely, we laughed with relief and exchanged a high five.

"Rosie, do you have any duct tape in that toolbox?" I asked.

"I do!" she replied, and tossed me a roll. I tore off a length and held my flashlight up to the pipes closest to the toggle switch, looking for anything unusual. After a few seconds, I spotted a white smudge on the underside of one of the pipes. I snapped a photo with my cell camera and carefully laid the strip over the area. When I removed the tape, the smudge came off with it. I sniffed the powder and immediately sneezed. Definitely not ectoplasm. It reminded me of sidewalk chalk. Folding the tape into a neat square, I stashed it in my pocket. I'd have George look at it later.

Rosie took her own strip of duct tape and secured the valve. Then we made our way out of the basement to survey the damage upstairs.

Though the rugs were soaked and a few books were waterlogged, we'd managed to cut off the flood before it reached the offices. Miss Irene's door was still closed, so we were going to have to break the news to her as gently as possible.

Rosie sighed. "Honestly, I'm grateful it wasn't worse. I just wish I knew a quicker way to dry out books."

"Don't worry. My friends and I will help. Maybe Victor will too. You could still make it home in time for dinner."

"That's sweet, Nancy, but books take days to dry out. And I'm soaking wet. Not great for date night," said Rosie sadly.

"You look good! Actually, your eye makeup looks even cooler now. I'm the one who's a mess."

"I can't leave Miss Irene to deal with this alone. She's barely hanging on as head librarian. If the board hears about it, they'll fire her, and maybe even put the property up for sale. Some of the trustees have wanted to sell for years, but Miss Irene always manages to convince the majority that the library should belong to the public. She's very persuasive when she wants to be. But then, so is Yvonne Coughlin."

I followed Rosie to the supply closet, where she took out a mop and bucket.

"She's developing the property next door, right?"

Rosie handed me a roll of paper towels, and I dried off as best I could.

"Yeah. Rich people think everything is for sale. I applied to a job with her company a couple of years ago, but Yvonne ended the interview as soon as I stepped through the door. Not pretty or rich enough for her, I guess."

"Well then, it's her loss. But hey, Rosie, are you okay to break the news about the flood to Miss Irene without me? I need to check on my friends."

"I'll be fine, don't worry. It won't be the first time I've given her bad news." She gave me a sad smile. "You better finish getting your cameras online while you have the chance. I'm really grateful you and your friends want to help. It's just been one thing after another this year, and apart from Miss Irene and me, nobody seems to care what happens to this dusty old library. But now we have you. Thanks for caring."

"Don't thank me yet. My friends and I are just starting our investigation."

"I can't wait to see what you can do," Rosie said. "You're a force!"

"Before you go, do you have something to write on?"

"Of course! I always have pencil and paper handy. It's part of the librarian's code." She took a pencil from the pocket of her jacket and passed it to me, along with a scrap from a small notebook she kept in the back pocket of her jeans.

"I'm giving you my cell number," I said as I wrote it on the paper. "Would you call me if anything else happens? Even with the cameras, it's good to have someone on the ground keeping an eye on things."

Rosie took back the scrap and her pencil. "You've got it, gumshoe."

I watched her approach Miss Irene's door, knock, and enter, before I limped back to the tower staircase, avoiding the wet spots, which on second glance looked like footprints. I slowly climbed the stairs, giving myself plenty of time to think. That flood would have been a perfect diversion if someone wanted to sneak into the tower room—or out of it. What was the ghost—or someone pretending to be the ghost—trying to find? Harriet's diary? If so, Ned was in big trouble, much worse than a scolding from a stern librarian.

I struggled to the top of the stairs, trying not to picture the worst, but when I entered the tower room, I was relieved to see Ned was safe and sound. He seemed to be frozen, hugging himself, presumably holding tight to Harriet's diary under his sweater. His surroundings were another matter. The room around him looked like it had been hit by a hurricane. I let out a low whistle, and I'm not usually a whistler.

Under other circumstances, I would've been amazed by the ornate ceiling and the stained-glass scenes of crows in flight, which filtered the sunlight into a silver-blue haze. The bookshelves were stocked with Coffin Hall's oldest and most precious volumes, and the low light made the gold lettering on their spines gleam and glimmer.

But instead my eyes were drawn to a flurry of torn, crumpled pages covering the floor. Books had been tossed from their shelves, the curtains had been ripped down, and someone had shattered the glass in several display cases. I also noticed a dusting of fine white powder on the ransacked cases and shelves. It looked just like the substance I'd found on the pipes in the basement. That meant the culprit who started the flood was probably the same one who trashed the tower room.

Ned's eyes were wide, and I could see he was breathing rapidly.

"Are you okay?" I asked. I limped over and wrapped my arms around him, but Ned just clutched himself tighter, his gaze fixed over my shoulder. I could feel the hard cover of the diary against his chest and how badly Ned wanted to keep it safe.

After a few seconds, he stopped shaking, and then, to my surprise, he began to laugh. "Wow, you stink, Nancy. And you're limping!"

"I'm fine. It's just a sprain. There was a small incident with the plumbing."

"What happened?"

"You first."

Ned sighed. "You're not going to believe me."

"Try me."

"I saw her again. Her face was scary pale. She really looked dead."

"The Blue Lady?"

Ned nodded.

"Is she . . . still here?" I asked, looking around for any flickers of movement.

"She's gone. I'm pretty sure she's gone."

"What's that stuff?" I asked, gesturing to the white-dusted shelves.

"Ectoplasm, I think," Ned replied. "It's a sort of residue ghosts leave behind."

"Hmm . . ." I ran my finger through the dust. It felt more like regular old powdered chalk than evidence of a ghost.

Ned cleared off one of the wooden chairs and helped me sit, still holding tight to the diary, then pulled up a chair across from me. "I heard noises as I was coming up the stairs, so when I reached the top, I hid behind the door and peeked inside. The place was already trashed, so she must have been at it for a while."

"I don't get it. Why is she so bent on destroying this room?"

Ned continued, ignoring my question. "She gave this awful scream. It was so loud, I thought the windows would shatter. I pressed myself up against the wall and tried to make myself invisible. It must have worked, because she flew past me and down the stairs, but I was too scared to follow her."

"Oh, Ned."

"I know how bad this looks. But she really *was* here. She did all this. And, Nancy—I think she was looking for something. I don't think Harriet's diary is safe at Coffin Hall."

"I'd have to agree with you there," I said.

Ned clutched the diary tighter.

"Okay, now you," he said.

"There was a flood downstairs. That's why you heard yelling. Rosie and I had to go down to the basement to fix it. It looked like someone had tampered with the pipes. And I found this."

I pulled out the tape with the white powder and

placed it on the table. "This chalk dust was in the basement. It looks just like the stuff on those shelves. I found it on a pipe right where someone might grab on for leverage while they switched the valves. Do you see what I'm getting at?"

"Not quite . . ."

"You said the ghost was deathly pale. You know what might make someone look that pale? Chalk!"

"Ohhh!" he exclaimed, holding up a torn page smudged with a chalky fingerprint.

"Here's what I'm wondering," I continued. "How did our ghost start the flood, destroy the tower room, and then escape, all without being seen by anyone but you?"

"Normal laws of physics don't apply to ghosts. They move in mysterious ways," Ned answered, only half-joking.

"Maybe, but a ghost doesn't leave wet footprints all along the hallway leading to the tower stairs. That's no mystery."

"All right, so let's say it's a person pretending to

be Harriet's ghost. It's not easy to get in and out right under Miss Irene's nose," Ned said.

"Exactly. The intruder would have to have help on the inside, knowledge of the security guards' schedule and which valves to turn to cause that flood . . ."

I heard voices drifting up the stairs—a disgusted squeal (that was Bess discovering the puddles), and then others: Miss Irene, Rosie, and an unknown male with a deeper voice than Victor's. I heard George call my name. We had about ten seconds before the others would make it up here and see the disaster. "Hide the diary," I whisper-shouted to Ned. "We'll smuggle it out again!"

Ned looked at me calmly. "It's okay," he said. "I'm going to come clean. All I can do is tell the truth. It's Miss Irene's job to keep the diary safe."

"Are you sure that's a good idea? I really hope you know what you're doing," I whispered just as George entered the room, followed by Bess and Rosie.

"Nancy, there you are!" George said, waving her hammer at me. "Two cameras down, one to go—oh!"

"Oh no," Rosie groaned. "More work for me."

CHAPTER SIX

A Trap Is Set

"I'M SO SORRY, ROSIE. THE BLUE LADY CAME back, and this time she meant business," I said.

"At least I managed to save this," Ned said, holding out Harriet's diary.

Rosie took it, shaking her head. Her round face was hard to read, but she stroked the book's cover like she was holding a kitten.

"To tell you the truth, I stole the diary the first time we were here, after the fire," Ned confessed. "That was wrong, and I shouldn't have done it. This afternoon I came back to return it to its rightful place, but the ghost was already here. I think she was looking for the diary to destroy it."

"Nancy, did you know about this?" Rosie asked.

I nodded, ashamed. "Ned took the diary by accident, and when I found out, I told him to bring it back right away," I explained, hoping Rosie would understand.

"It's true!" Bess chimed in.

"I'm telling you, Ned didn't make this mess," I said.

Rosie frowned, thinking it over. "Silly me. I thought a volunteer gig at a library would be easy and stress-free. I'm devastated that we haven't been able to keep our collection safe from . . . whoever she is."

We heard voices from the stairwell—Miss Irene's, and the male voice I didn't recognize. In a few seconds, the librarian would see the destroyed books and the stolen diary and probably ban us from Coffin Hall for life.

"Okay, here's what we'll do. Hide the diary," Rosie told Ned. "You're right. It isn't safe here. Take it home with you and keep it somewhere out of sight until we can figure out what's going on. I'll cover for you with Miss Irene and Terry as best I can."

Ned tucked the diary into the waistband of his pants and covered it with his shirt, then zipped his jacket over it. Just in time, because at that moment Miss Irene entered the tower room, closely followed by a thin, long-faced man with a gray ponytail and a soul patch. He wore a security uniform that looked several sizes too large for him, and a belt with a heavy black flashlight, a walkie-talkie, and a huge ring of keys. This must be Terry, the senior security guard, fresh from his vacation. What a scene to come back to!

There was a moment of stunned silence as they took the mess in. Then Miss Irene spoke, and though her voice sounded calm, I could tell she was barely holding back her anger.

"Don't tell me. Another visit from the Blue Lady. And once again, Nancy Drew and Ned Nickerson are at the center of it."

"Would you like me to call the police, ma'am?" asked Terry. His deep, rich voice didn't match his ill-fitting uniform or his aging hippie hairstyle. It was the voice of a newscaster or a train conductor, someone with authority, someone people trusted.

"Absolutely not," she said. "If I call the police, the board will be notified, and they'll shut us down tomorrow. No, we'll have to handle this internally. Rosie, please tell me Harriet's diary is safe."

"Yes, it's fine. I have it," Rosie said innocently.

I decided to get out ahead of any accusations Miss Irene might make. "Miss Irene, I believe someone may be impersonating Harriet Coffin to damage the library's collection. I don't know why they're doing it, but it's the only explanation that makes sense."

"Hmm," Miss Irene said, clearly unimpressed. "How about instead of sitting around coming up with wild theories, you all help me clean up this mess. Mr. Nickerson, you can start by gathering up all the pages. . . ."

I checked my phone—it was after six o'clock. This room had been through a lot in one day. Rosie brought over a cart for reshelving, and George and Bess began retrieving books from the floor.

The security guard approached me.

"Miss Drew, I'm Terry Vila. It's a pleasure. I've heard all about you. You are a legend in my community." Terry enunciated every word carefully, as though he were onstage.

I heard Ned make a strangled noise, like he wanted to say something but had stopped himself. Terry held out his hand for me to shake. I took it. He had a limp handshake, and I could tell he didn't enjoy touching people.

"Oh? What community is that?"

"Ghost hunters. We admired your work at Grey Fox Inn, the haunted hotel in Charleston. I'm from New Orleans myself, and let me tell you, some ghosts are as real as you and me. The Blue Lady is one of them."

"Really?" I said, raising an eyebrow. "I might have to disagree with you there."

"Yes. In fact, I saw her tonight, just as I was driving up the hill. She was floating across the grounds by the cemetery, lit up like a Christmas tree."

"No you didn't, Terry," Miss Irene scolded him. "Stop making up stories. This isn't your podcast."

"Oh my gosh! Terry, it *is* you!" Ned cut in. "I thought I recognized your voice right away but wasn't sure. Sorry, I'm Ned—I'm a big fan. *Tales from the Haunted Library* inspired me to come to Coffin Hall to look at Harriet's diary. I had no idea you worked here."

"Terry, I told you that publicity would do us no favors," Miss Irene said, looking annoyed.

"You know there's no such thing as bad publicity, Miss Irene," Terry replied. "As I say on *Tales from the Haunted Library*, energy attracts energy. It's the strongest force in the universe. Thanks for listening, young man. It means the world to this old ghost chaser."

Ned blushed. "I like how you present the facts about each ghost sighting. You get such good stories from your sources, too. You know how to ask the right questions. I admire that. I've been working on a podcast of my own called *NED Talks*—"

"Might want to rethink that name," Terry said, chuckling.

But Ned continued as if he hadn't heard. "I guess I was trying to pick up the investigation where you left off. I thought I could find out what happened to Harriet and her family's fortune. I had no idea what I was getting myself into."

Miss Irene sighed as she smoothed out page after crumpled page on the tabletop. "It takes years to build something as valuable as this library, and only a few minutes to tear it down."

"Please don't tell me we have to take the cameras down now," George said testily. "It took forever to get them online."

"No, we need them more than ever," I replied. "And anyway, I think I know how to attract some attention to the library's problems without bringing the board into it."

"Ask for forgiveness, not permission, I always say," Terry chimed in. Miss Irene frowned.

"What's your plan, Nancy?" Ned asked.

"The Blue Lady still hasn't found whatever it is she was looking for. I'll bet she comes back to search again in the next couple of days. All we have to do is wait, right? If we take shifts, we can keep an eye on the cameras twenty-four seven."

"I don't know about you guys, but I have other things to do besides ghost watching," Bess objected.

"What if we crowdsource the hunt?" Ned suggested. "Make the streams public and let people online help us spot the Blue Lady. If we get enough viewers, it'll be like having an automatic ghost-alert system. We can add notifications, so the minute she's spotted, we'll know and can alert Victor or Terry."

"Great idea," I said, flashing Ned a grin.

"Ooh yes!" George rubbed her hands together. "I can add a screenshot feature so viewers can submit their evidence. We can call the livestream Coffin Online . . . or the Specter in the Stacks!"

Miss Irene shook her head. "I don't see how making our problems public will help. You don't know who's out there or what their intentions might be. I may not be a tech expert, but I've heard of Photoshop and deepfakes. This whole effort could easily spiral out of control."

"Leave that to me," Terry answered smoothly. "I know the ins and outs of the internet almost as well as I know Coffin Hall."

I didn't totally trust the guy, but I appreciated him supporting our plan, especially because Miss Irene knew and trusted him.

"I'm plugged in to the online ghost-hunting community," Terry went on. "If I post about the livestream on my accounts, we'll have no trouble attracting experienced viewers—folks who've spent their whole lives searching for spirits. Catching the fake Blue Lady, if she is fake, should be easy for them."

Miss Irene surveyed us carefully, considering her options.

I met her gaze and spoke calmly, making my case: "Miss Irene, as you've said, Coffin Hall is full of history and information, and it's beautiful here too. But nobody knows this place exists. If we livestream the feed, more people will be invested in what happens to the library. That means more patrons, and more patrons mean the board might stop trying to shut you down. The Blue Lady could actually help you protect Coffin Hall, just as Harriet intended."

Miss Irene buried her face in her hands. "How did it come to this? Relying on social media to save us," she murmured, mostly to herself.

Rosie rubbed her back. "It'll be all right, Miss Irene. And it wouldn't be such a bad thing to bring Coffin Hall into the twenty-first century."

"Fine," she said, after a long moment. "I suppose I'm desperate enough to try this."

"I've actually been working to digitize some of William's letters in my spare time," Rosie confessed. "They're on a thumb drive in my desk."

"You've been sneaking into my office?" Miss Irene said, horrified. "Where did you get the key to my cabinet?"

Rosie bit her lip before answering. "I had a copy made one day when you were out to lunch. I was going to surprise you with the collection when it was complete. Imagine how much easier it'll be to study Harriet and William's code and make connections we couldn't see before!"

Miss Irene huffed. "I don't know whether to be angry with you for breaking into my office and horning in on my research or proud of you for taking the initiative. Rosie, what did I do to deserve you?"

Rosie smiled angelically. "I don't know, but you're stuck with me now. You couldn't pay me to go away."

"I don't pay you to stay, either."

"I can't help it," Rosie said. "I love this spooky place, and I know you love it too. But Miss Irene, it's not wrong to ask for help sometimes."

Miss Irene blinked back a tear. Rosie's words had touched her. Even so, she spoke briskly. "The mess is cleaned up enough for now. Let's go home for the night and let Terry and the cameras take it from here."

"That sounds good," said Rosie. "I can't wait to get home and start painting."

"Will you bring us the thumb drive before you go?" I asked.

"Sure. I'll be right back!"

"Terry, would you follow me back on social media?" Ned asked sheepishly. "Then I can DM you the link for the ghost cams."

Terry nodded. "What's your handle?"

I rolled my eyes. *Podcast bros.*

"Uh, I'm NedTalksPod77."

"NedTalksPod76 was taken?" George quipped.

"Seven just so happens to be my favorite number, and two sevens are better than one."

"Sound reasoning," Terry said, tapping at his phone. "There. Followed."

"Promise you won't let fame change you," I said, teasing.

Ned laughed, then took my hand and looked deep into my eyes. "I promise I'll always be your Ned, no matter what."

"I know you will," I said, giving him a quick peck on the cheek.

"Aw," cooed Bess.

George rolled her eyes. "You mean *ew*."

Rosie raced back up the stairs and handed me a thumb drive decorated with little skulls in bright colors. "The first batch of letters is on here. I've been working on an index of symbol combinations, so you can see every time a combination is used. I thought it might be helpful for identifying commonly used words. I put that on the drive for you too."

"Thanks, Rosie. It seems like you've thought of everything." I turned to face Miss Irene. "We'll do everything we can to catch this vandal."

"Please call me the moment you find anything," Miss Irene said.

"Of course. All right, gang. It's time for the Blue Lady to get her fifteen minutes of internet fame."

CHAPTER SEVEN

On Shaky Ground

MY FRIENDS AND I DIDN'T TALK MUCH AS we made our way down the stone steps of Coffin Hall and entered the parking lot. I was worried that Miss Irene or Terry would discover that we had the diary and send the police after us.

Ned, George, Bess, and I all piled into my car and pulled away from Coffin Hall just as the sun sank below the horizon. George had her laptop open and was already downloading Rosie's scans of the letters. Bess was texting with Rosie. In the rearview mirror, I saw Terry join Rosie and Miss Irene on the front steps to see us off. I was uneasy about leaving him in charge of the next stage of our plan, but Miss Irene seemed to trust him, so I tried to ignore my doubts, which was near impossible. After all, a detective is supposed to trust her intuition.

The Blue Lady had been roaming Coffin Hall a long time before she became destructive, but it seemed like Terry hadn't done much more than use the recent incidents as material for his podcast. For a moderately famous ghost hunter, he didn't seem like a very good investigator. I wanted to hear that episode of *Tales from the Haunted Library* for myself.

"Hey, Ned, can you put on Terry's episode about Harriet?"

"Yeah, hang on," he said, searching his phone. He shifted in his seat, checking the mirrors every few seconds as if he expected to find the Blue Lady tailing us.

"I like how you called her Harriet, like she's our friend," Bess said from the back seat.

"I'd like to think we would get along, if we'd ever had the chance to meet," I replied. "She and I both love secrets and intrigue."

"Here it is!" said Ned, hitting play.

I drove along the stately driveway, passing through the grounds of the Coffin estate as shadows raced across the grass. I couldn't help thinking they looked like ghostly fingers. Spending all day (more or less) at Coffin Hall had done weird things to my mind.

Terry's molasses-slow voice filtered through the speakers. "Welcome to the fire, wanderers. It's quiet out there tonight. Too quiet. Have a seat and listen, but don't ever let your guard down. You don't know what might come through the static. This is . . . *Tales from the Haunted Library*. I'm Terry Vila, your voice in the darkness, broadcasting from my secret underground lair."

George snorted. "A secret underground lair? More like his mom's basement. Do people actually take this guy seriously?"

"His research is solid," Ned protested.

Terry's voice droned on. "Tonight I'll introduce you to someone very close to my heart. Harriet Coffin was tall, beautiful, witty, and most importantly, rich. She was the sole heir of Hieronymous Zenas Coffin, a noted water baron, landlord, and commercial developer who transformed the hamlet of River Heights into a bustling agricultural center in just a few decades.

"Harriet was River Heights's most eligible bachelorette. You could say she lit up the room . . . but her sinister surname sealed her fate. Her family's blood feud may have been the reason for her mysterious disappearance and untimely, unknown death."

There was some ominous music and the sound of a knife slicing through the air, followed by a woman screaming, and then a large splash, like something heavy falling into fast-moving water.

"A bit much for a history podcast, don't you think?" Bess said.

"The dramatizations are kind of cringeworthy," Ned admitted.

Terry continued his story: "Harriet's spirit now haunts the tower room of Coffin Hall. The identity of the person who may have killed her is a mystery, as is the cause of her death and the location of her family fortune. Harriet's secret diary may be the key to the whole mystery, but it's written in an impenetrable code. . . ."

My headlights passed over the Coffin family grave-yard, and I couldn't help pulling over for one last look at Harriet's monument. Something was different. There was still no water running into its basin, but now the fountain appeared to be leaning slightly to the right, as though the ground beneath was sinking. Other grave-stones nearby were tilting too, and a few had even toppled over. What was happening under the Coffin estate?

"Why are we stopping?" George asked. "Don't tell me you forgot something at the library!"

"Seriously, Nancy," Ned said. "I'd really like to get off the Coffin property as soon as possible."

"This won't take more than a minute, I promise," I said, putting the car in park and turning off the engine. I climbed out of the car and waved for Ned to join me, but he shook his head.

"I'd rather wait in the car, if that's okay with you," he replied. George, however, jumped out and eagerly bounded after me.

We started across the grounds, picking through the

brambly, overgrown field toward the graveyard fence, using my phone flashlight to light the way. Maybe my eyes were playing tricks on me, but Harriet's fountain seemed to tilt over more and more as I approached, as though the earth was in the process of swallowing it up. On the other side of the cemetery, the chain-link construction fence had also begun to sag in the middle.

I should've taken these details as a warning. Instead I walked faster, not paying much attention to where I stepped. Suddenly I felt the ground under me give way. My legs plunged knee-deep into mud. George let out a yell of surprise, and Ned and Bess came running.

The more I struggled, the deeper I sank. Coffin Hall wasn't ready to let me go yet, not by a long shot.

A few moments later, Ned and George had grabbed hold of my arms and were hauling me out of the muck. Bess backed them up with an old beach towel, ready to wrap it around me.

"Ned, you saved me!" I exclaimed when I'd managed to catch my breath. Usually, I was the one rescuing him from kidnappers or smugglers.

"Excuse me," George protested. "I helped too!"

"Okay, George. You're also my hero."

She crossed her arms. "*Thank* you."

Between the library dust, the sewer water, and now this mud, my clothes were done for. But where had the mud come from? When I'd walked to the cemetery earlier, the ground had been solid. It hadn't rained since then, and I didn't see any sign of a sprinkler system or anything like that. How could the ground become so unstable so quickly? Maybe it was connected to the flood in the library. . . .

I still wanted to get a closer look at that construction site's wonky fence, which was now sagging so much it would be easy to hop over. I stood, brushed myself off, and, ignoring my friends' protests, cautiously made my way toward the chain link. Ned urged me to be careful as he followed on my heels.

When I reached the fence, I spotted some sort of flat white object trampled into the mud. Several sets of footprints crossed it. More than one person had passed over the fence from the construction site to the

Coffin Hall grounds recently. Terry had said he'd seen the Blue Lady near the cemetery, but ghosts don't leave footprints. Who had he really seen?

I knelt and freed a corner of the object, which was pierced with metal grommets. I realized it was a sign that must have once been attached to the chain link. After wiping at the mud coating the board with the sleeve of my already filthy sweater, I could make out large red letters forming the words COUGHLIN CAPITAL: FOR THE PEOPLE.

"Oh, give me a break," I muttered, snapping a flash photo with my phone. Nothing I'd learned about Coughlin Capital so far made me think they were developing this project to help people. The sign was little more than a marketing campaign to convince someone that Yvonne Coughlin's business empire served a higher cause.

I then noticed a scrap of fabric sticking out from beneath the sign. Pulling it out, I saw that it was a once-white cotton bag with a strap. I wrinkled my nose as I felt around inside—empty—but when I pulled my hand out, it was covered in white powder. More chalk!

"What do you think this is for?" I asked my friends.

"No idea, Nance," George said. "It looks like trash to me."

"Is that the same chalk we found in the tower room?" Ned asked.

"That chalk bag looks just like the ones we used to use for gymnastics class," Bess chimed in. "You put the chalk on your hands to help you grip better. Mountain climbers use it too."

"Interesting, and there's a logo on here," I said as I cleared some of the mud from the fabric. "I'd better hang on to this. I wonder if the chalk explains the Blue Lady's pale appearance. It can't be a coincidence that we found this on Yvonne Coughlin's construction site."

"You're not thinking of jumping that fence, are you, Nancy?" Ned asked, sounding anxious.

"Am I that easy to read?" I asked, flashing him a bright smile. "I want to know what's going on beneath Coffin Hall. If I climb down into the area they were excavating this morning, maybe I can find some clues."

"Yeah . . . but it's dark, Nancy," Ned said. "You just fell into a sinkhole. What if they have security or Yvonne Coughlin drops by? All I want to do now is go home, have a hot chocolate, and go to bed early."

"Hear, hear!" said George.

A pair of headlights coming from Coffin Hall cut through the darkness. The beat-up station wagon slowed as it drew up beside my hybrid. Then the passenger-side window rolled down and I heard Rosie call my name.

"I thought you'd be halfway home by now! What are you doing out here in the dark? Are you . . . covered in mud?"

"Curiosity got the best of me," I replied with a small shrug. "Look at Harriet's fountain and the fence: everything's sinking! When I tried to get a better look, suddenly I was sinking too!"

"Oh my gosh. It's good your friends were here to pull you out. And now you know why the Coffin Hall grounds aren't a popular picnic spot."

"Do these fields flood often?"

"Anytime it rains or snows or it's even a bit misty

in the morning. Personally, I think the plumbing is to blame. There used to be a huge orchard here. Hieronymous Coffin grew almonds, but the trees aren't native to the Midwest, so they're really high maintenance and super thirsty. Hieronymous had his gardeners build special tents for the trees to keep them warm in the winter. And in the summer, he had to keep them really well watered. It takes, like, two thousand gallons of water to produce a pound of almonds. Some people think Hieronymous found a way to pump water straight from the river so he didn't have to pay taxes to the county, but I've never seen any evidence of that in the library's records."

"That guy sounds like he was a piece of work," Ned said. "All the money in the world, and he couldn't be bothered to give even a little bit of it back to his community."

Rosie chuckled. "Rich people are cheap. How else do you think they got rich in the first place? They negotiate sweet deals for themselves, then turn around and charge everyone else an arm and a leg."

"The cycle continues," I said, pointing toward the fallen Coughlin Capital sign.

"'For the people'?" Rosie read, then hooted with laughter. "Whew, that's a good one. Oh, Yvonne, never change."

"I saw Yvonne at the construction site earlier today," I said. "She wants to buy Coffin Hall, but so far the city won't go for it. Do you think Yvonne would take drastic measures to get what she wants?"

Rosie considered the question for a moment. "Maybe, but Yvonne is a smart cookie. She knows how to keep her hands clean. I don't think she'd do anything that extreme on her own."

"Good to know. Thanks."

"Anytime! Now, I really do have to go. My partner's been painting for hours. He's probably covered the whole canvas by now. Keep me posted on the ghost cams, though! You've got my number."

"Yes, will do. Good night!"

She flashed us a *rock on* sign and drove off into the night. I gave the Coughlin construction site one last glance, but in the dark, I couldn't see much worth investigating. Resolving to return tomorrow, I took Bess's towel and laid it over my driver's seat, and then we all climbed back into the car.

"I can't wait to get back on Wi-Fi," George said. "For all we know, the Blue Lady could be waltzing around Coffin Hall arm in arm with Terry right now."

"Also, if we don't leave now, I'm pretty sure our souls will be trapped at Coffin Hall for all eternity," Ned added with a nervous laugh.

"All right, all right. But first thing tomorrow, I'm coming back," I said.

We zoomed past the guardhouse and through Coffin Hall's iron gate as if a ghost was chasing us.

And who knows? Maybe she was.

CHAPTER EIGHT

Biblioghost

BACK AT MY HOUSE, HANNAH WAS ALREADY setting out a delicious late dinner, and fortunately, she'd made more than enough for everyone. I urged my friends to start eating and excused myself to wash off the day's grime and ice my throbbing ankle. I also did a quick internet search of the logo on the chalk bag and found it was made by a company that sold high-end mountain-climbing gear. Interesting.

When I returned to the dining room, Hannah handed me a plate of pot roast she'd been keeping warm for me. Everyone else had finished eating, and Ned had already filled my dad in on the day's events. Dad was shaking his head in disbelief.

"Ghosts, fires, vandalism, flash floods, sinkholes, and secret codes—sounds like Coffin Hall pulled out all the stops for you kids. You must be exhausted. Other than getting Ned out of trouble with that librarian, all I've done today is organize some files and make a couple of phone calls."

"Just another day in the life of a young detective," I said, bringing my fork to my mouth. "I can't help it if my life is more exciting than yours."

George had her laptop out. On the screen, I could see three grainy shots of a darkened Coffin Hall. "So far, nothing. No Blue Lady, and no sign of Terry, either," she said.

"I sent him the link to the streams," Ned said. "He hasn't posted on the *Haunted Library* accounts yet, but I'm sure he will soon. They're up on my account, but I only have fourteen followers, so they haven't gotten many views yet."

"I decided on a name for the stream," George said. "*Biblioghost!*"

"That's not bad," I replied. "Pretty catchy."

"Thank you!" George grinned. "I'm working on a graphic for the website now."

She turned her screen to face me. The word *Biblioghost* was made out of books, with a little cartoon spirit escaping through the second *O*.

"That's so cool!" Ned said. "Except that ghost doesn't look anything like the Blue Lady."

George raised an eyebrow. "Artistic license."

"But how will the viewers know what to look for?"

"I'm no ghost hunter," Dad interjected, "but in a manhunt, it's actually better if the public doesn't know every detail about the suspect. If police tell people too much about what to expect, they can get carried away and report things they didn't actually see. If you keep some details in reserve, it's easier to sort out the real reports from the fake ones."

"Dessert!" Hannah announced, carrying a lemon pound cake with royal icing to the table. She cut us each a slice and passed the plates around.

"Ooh, Hannah, this looks delicious. Thank you!" I said. Ned devoured his slice in two bites. Bess ate slowly and daintily, savoring every crumb. George barely touched hers, which was not like her at all. Usually, George inhaled her dessert even faster than Ned.

"We're up to eleven viewers now," George said, eyes fixed on her laptop. "Twelve, thirteen, fourteen, fifteen, twenty! Did Terry post something on his podcast account?"

"Let me check," Ned said, scrolling through his phone. "Hmm. Not yet."

"All organic growth. Cool!" George said. "What if we go viral? We could become ghost influencers . . . ghostfluencers. I'm all in on ghost wordplay now, and I'm not going to apologize."

"Can you explain to me how this webcam idea is supposed to work?" Dad asked.

"In order to debunk the ghost story the suspect is playing into, we have to find evidence that she's not actually a ghost," I replied. "This footage might give us clues about how she's breaking in."

"I understand that part. I guess I'm less comfortable that you're turning the investigation over to random strangers on the internet. The public can't always be trusted."

"You sound just like Miss Irene," George pouted. "By the way, we're up to thirty viewers now."

I gave my dad a shrug. "I guess I believe in the power of the internet to do good sometimes."

"I'm not a technophobe. I just want you to be careful. Make sure you examine all the angles before you believe something you read online."

My dad is a great lawyer, and sometimes he turns his interrogation skills on me, pointing out holes in my logic or problems with my evidence. I don't always appreciate the critique, but I'm a much better detective for it.

"Oh look, there's Terry!" George turned her screen so the rest of us could see it and pointed to the main lobby camera feed. A pixelated figure crossed the screen from left to right. I recognized Terry's uniform and flashlight beam. He came across the screen again, running his light along the lobby's curved walls.

"At least we know he's really on duty and not just sitting around," I said.

"Mr. Drew, do you mind if I use your scanner?" Bess asked. She was gently holding Harriet's diary in her arms.

"Of course, but may I ask why?"

"One of the library volunteers digitized some of William's letters. They're written in the same code as Harriet's diary." Bess opened the diary to show Dad a few of the pages. "If we scan in the diary, we can search for phrases and words that repeat. It might help us break the code."

"Oh right. The famous diary." Dad chuckled. "A lot of time and effort has been wasted trying to read that young lady's diary."

"A waste of time?" Bess sputtered. "Is it a waste of time to tell Harriet's true story? All her life, her father tried to tell her who she was and how to live. This diary might have been the only place where she could be herself."

"I'm sorry, Bess. I didn't mean to sound callous," Dad replied. "It would be amazing if you girls were the ones to crack her code. But decoding the diary won't help you catch the person who's been attacking Coffin Hall."

"That may be true," I said, "but I'm starting to think the historical details might be key to solving this case. Whoever is breaking into Coffin Hall has been searching for something, and I'm pretty sure they want Harriet's diary."

My dad seemed satisfied with my explanation, because he gave Bess the okay to use his office. Bess thanked him and dragged George out of the room to start the painstaking process of scanning Harriet's spidery handwriting.

"Forty-two viewers!" George yelled on her way out the door. "We're blowing up!"

Ned and I were left alone with Dad. I pulled up the photo of the Coughlin Capital sign on my phone and showed it to him. "What do you make of this?"

"Hah! Notice the sign doesn't say *which* people. With the Coughlins, there are always the right and wrong sorts of people."

"You know Yvonne Coughlin?"

"I've tussled with her lawyers on behalf of more than a few clients. Her development company has a habit of overstepping property lines, but her lawyers are just as ruthless as they are expensive. I haven't managed to beat them in court once. In my experience, you do not say no to Yvonne Coughlin."

"That's what I've been hearing . . . ," I said.

George burst back into the room with her laptop balanced in one hand and her phone in the other. Bess was right behind her.

"Six hundred viewers! *Biblioghost* is a hit!" George shouted.

"A few minutes ago, you were at forty-two!" Ned exclaimed, nearly jumping out of his seat. "What happened? Is this because Terry posted to his podcast accounts?"

George was banging away at the keyboard, jumping

between windows at lightning speed. "I haven't had time to confirm it, but it must be. Bess and I were in the middle of scanning. I glanced over to check the feed and saw this huge spike. I'm getting reports from viewers every minute. Nothing worthwhile yet, but if we have this many people watching, it won't be long before they spot something."

"Here, George. Take my seat," Dad said. "I'm heading up to bed. Nancy, you can fill me in over breakfast tomorrow. Actually, make it brunch. I'm sleeping in."

I kissed my dad good night.

"Good luck with the ghost hunt," he said, pausing in the doorway. "Promise me you won't stay up all night watching the feed."

"I promise," I said, knowing I probably would. I heard him climbing the stairs. Hannah had left a light on in the kitchen, but the rest of the house was already dark.

George and Bess pulled up chairs and we all huddled around the laptop. George took a sip of my dad's old coffee, then pulled a face.

"Let me pull up Terry's account and see what he said." I opened my phone and found the *Tales from the Haunted Library* Twitter account. Sure enough, Terry had posted a link to the *Biblioghost* stream a few minutes before. But I gasped when I saw what else he'd posted. Instead of boosting the page, he'd written a long thread claiming *Biblioghost* as his own investigation.

"'Some of you may remember the story of Harriet Coffin, the Blue Lady, from way back in season one,'" I read aloud. "'Now I am leading the investigation into the strange occurrences at Coffin Hall with my viral livestream, *Biblioghost*.'"

"What?" George was outraged. "Why is he trying to take credit for our investigation? This was one hundred percent our idea! And I did all the work of installing the cameras!"

"Come on, George, it's not the end of the world," Bess said, trying to calm her down. "You know *I* think you're a genius."

I read his next tweet in the thread: "The Blue Lady's energy is dark. Threatening. Who knows what she's capable of? Stay tuned to *Biblioghost*, and beware.'"

George grabbed my phone and let out an angry yelp.

"The post already has three hundred likes!"

Ned tried his best to calm her down. "I mean, at least Terry's getting the information out there. And none of us asked to be credited. The important thing is collecting evidence."

"I guess," George pouted. "But I built this streaming page from scratch, and I designed the logo. I don't like that he's trying to take credit for my work."

"I totally hear you," I replied. "What Terry did was wrong, but Ned is right. The evidence is the most important thing right now. As long as we get what we need to catch the ghost impostor, clear Ned's name, and protect Coffin Hall from more 'hauntings,' it doesn't really matter who gets the credit."

"Terry may be self-centered, but he's one of the good guys," Ned added.

"You're just a fanboy," Bess teased. "Admit it."

"Okay, maybe I'm biased, but I really think he's on our side," Ned replied.

I wasn't as certain. "I hope that's the case. Some people like solving mysteries for the fame and the attention. That's not why I do this. I just want to find the truth."

Terry had already lied once to impress his followers. What else could he lie about?

"Please give him a chance," Ned insisted. "I've listened to all his episodes. He's smart. He always tells the whole story. Maybe he thought taking credit for *Biblioghost* was the best way to make sure people paid attention."

"What's the viewer count now, George?" I asked.

"We're at three thousand . . . thirty-one hundred . . . thirty-one fifty. . . . The number keeps going up. I think we actually *are* going viral," George replied, her eyes wide.

"How do you want to go through all these incoming ghost reports? Should we take it in shifts?" Bess asked.

"Yeah, good idea," I replied. "George, you take first watch. Bess, you take second, I'll take third, and if nothing happens overnight, we can get Ned up at six to take over."

Ned grumbled a little about getting the early shift, but he agreed.

"Bess and I can stay up together," George said. "I don't think I could fall asleep tonight anyway."

"We were going to keep scanning the diary to check the code against Rosie's symbol database. George said I could crash at her place. Is it okay if we hang on to the diary to finish scanning it?"

"I don't see why not," I replied. "Ned, any objections?"

"No, I think George and Bess can keep it safe for one night."

Bess started gathering her things. "I'll call you before we go to bed, Nance."

"Thanks, guys."

"We've got this," George said.

"Hey, don't get too confident," I cautioned. "After the day she's had, who knows when the Blue Lady will show herself again?"

CHAPTER NINE

~

Late-Night Visitors

AS GEORGE HAD PREDICTED, IT WAS impossible to fall asleep. I couldn't stop replaying everything that had happened at Coffin Hall that day, hoping I might remember some detail that could help identify the Blue Lady impersonator. As I opened my window to let in some fresh air, I wondered if Ned was still lying awake too.

I resisted the urge to check the *Biblioghost* page or my phone for updates from Bess and George. I'd turned up the ringer so my phone would wake me if they called anyway.

After a while, I must have dozed off, because I found myself standing in front of the mysterious door in the Coffin Hall basement. In my dream, light shone through the crack around the door, and I could hear the faint sound of someone whistling an old-fashioned tune, a waltz. The whistling grew louder, then stopped, only to be followed by the click of the lock opening. The door swung open on well-oiled hinges, and a woman stepped through, gathering up her tasseled skirt to keep it from getting wet, which was completely unnecessary since she was floating several inches off the ground. Her face was very pale and her eyes dark and sunken, like those of a skull. The metal door swung shut with a *clang*, trapping me in the basement with the apparition. I opened my mouth to scream, but no sound came out.

The Blue Lady's mouth didn't move, but somehow I heard her whispering as though she were speaking directly into my ear. Her voice was scratchy, as if it hadn't been used in a hundred years.

Where is my diary? she said. The ghost came closer, and I felt a wave of intense cold pass through my entire body. Even though I knew I was dreaming, the voice and the chill felt real. I was too petrified to respond. I tried to tell my brain to wake up, but the cold only grew more intense.

The Blue Lady repeated her question, growing angry. *Where have you hidden it, little girl? What gives you the right to keep it from me? The diary is mine! Give it here, quickly, or I swear I will ruin you!*

No matter which way I turned, the tangle of pipes blocked my escape. I searched for a gap, but the web only grew denser. Then, suddenly, the pipes all sprang a leak and the basement quickly filled with water. It didn't seem to affect the ghost. She loomed over me as I splashed and struggled, her ghastly grin growing and growing until it was wide enough to swallow me whole.

A high-pitched electronic jingle cut through the roar of rushing water. My phone!

I opened my eyes and the nightmare dissolved. It took me a second to get my bearings. I was in my bedroom, safe and warm under the covers, and there was no ghost. The only blue glow was coming from my phone screen, which displayed Bess's number and the time, 4:30 a.m.

Though I desperately wanted to answer, something told me to stay still a moment longer. I sensed movement near my window, realizing with a rush of horror that I really wasn't alone. There was a swishing sound like the rustle of skirts. Was the Blue Lady here after all? Maybe I was still dreaming. I rubbed my eyes hard and blinked to clear my vision. In the dark I could make out a person trying to climb out over my windowsill. The intruder's gown seemed to be caught on the frame. They were kicking frantically, trying to free the fabric, and in the moonlight, I saw they were wearing a pair of sensible clogs. Very un-ghostlike.

I grabbed my phone and hit record as I jumped out of bed, ready to grab for the intruder's ankles if I had to.

"Stop right there!" I yelled. "I've got you on camera! Dad! Dad, come quick, there's someone in my room!"

In their rush to get away, the intruder tore their

skirt free and swung their feet over the sill, leaving a long strip of fabric behind.

An engine revved, a car door slammed, and tires squealed. All I saw was the glow of taillights as the getaway car peeled out of our street and turned onto the main road.

I hadn't gotten a good look at the intruder's face, and all my camera had captured was a blur moving across the screen. Did this person want me to believe they were a ghost too? If so, they'd spoiled their own illusion. Ghosts don't need a getaway car or a driver. This intruder was alive, and they weren't acting alone.

I inspected the windowsill and the ground below my window with my phone flashlight, but there was no sign of the chalky substance I'd found at the scene of other Blue Lady apparitions. Wait until Bess and George heard about my surprise visitor.

Bess picked up on the first ring. "Nancy, you'll never believe this. We have the Blue Lady live on camera in the library lobby right now. She's . . . um . . . she's posing for us."

"But Bess . . . she was just *here*. I dreamed she was here, searching for her diary. You two still have it, right?"

"What? Wait, hang on. I'm putting you on speaker. Okay, say that again."

"I was having a nightmare about the Blue Lady. Then I woke up, and someone dressed as the Blue Lady was actually here in my bedroom! I tried to stop them, but they escaped out the window."

"Oh my gosh! Are you okay?" Bess asked.

"I'm fine, but I'm worried about Ned. If that midnight intruder could find my address, they could just as easily find Ned's, and George's, too. There could be more Blue Ladies climbing through your windows right this moment."

George groaned. "I can barely handle one ghost!"

"We tried to get through to Terry, but our calls have been going straight to voice mail," Bess added. "I think he has his phone on Do Not Disturb."

"A security guard who doesn't want to be disturbed. Nothing shady about that," said George sarcastically.

"It doesn't look great for Terry," I agreed. "But what's going on with *Biblioghost*?"

"It's unreal," said George. "I can see the Blue Lady perfectly—everything but her face. She's wearing some kind of veil. She's there, Nancy, and she's really glowing, or the dress is anyway."

"It could be fiber-optics," Bess mused. "The dress, I mean. Charli Manes wore a fiber-optic dress to the Oscars last year. It's made with this special fabric that lights up and can even change color. That dress is really expensive, obviously, otherwise I'd totally buy one."

"Put me on hold and check the link yourself," George said. "Here, I'm texting it to you."

I pulled up the *Biblioghost* page on my phone. Sure enough, the main lobby feed showed a grainy, shimmering figure moving around the space. This Blue Lady was putting on a show, striking poses and playing to the camera. As the Blue Lady passed under the light from the emergency exit sign, I spotted something that proved she wasn't supernatural—she cast a shadow against the wall.

"That's no ghost," I said.

"Yeah, no kidding," said George.

"How did this person know about the cameras? We just installed them. The only ones who saw us do it were Miss Irene, Rosie, and Terry. Terry, who isn't answering his phone . . ." That fact alone had put him at the top of my suspect list, along with Yvonne Coughlin.

"The *Biblioghost* viewers are angry," said George. "They're saying *Biblioghost* is a setup. One guy thinks we're doing a viral marketing campaign. Someone else claims we're filming a reality show. They're hard-core ghost hunters, and they think we are trying to make them look stupid."

"George, I hate to say this, but you have to shut down the feeds. With the ghost hunters against us, we can't keep *Biblioghost* going now."

George wailed. "I worked so hard!"

"We won't get any useful evidence now. It's over," I said. "I'm sorry, George."

"So it's a conspiracy?" George asked.

"If it is, it's not a very good one. All these different

ghosts seem to want different things. This Blue Lady is mugging for the camera, but the Blue Lady who set the fire in the tower room didn't want to be seen. I can't tell whether the Blue Lady wants to protect Harriet's diary or destroy it. Where's the diary right now?"

"Bess has it under her pillow."

"That's not a good enough hiding place. Can you meet me at Ned's? If Terry isn't going to protect Coffin Hall, we'll have to go up there ourselves."

"Can do. As long as you don't mind us showing up in pajamas."

I laughed, but I was still a little shaken from my own surprise encounter. Bess must have picked up on my distress.

"I'm sure Ned's perfectly fine," she said kindly.

"Yeah, he's probably snoring away right now, totally clueless," George added.

"I'd rather not take any chances," I replied. "If the shadowy forces behind the Blue Lady have gotten desperate enough to break into people's houses, they're not going to leave any stones unturned."

We hung up and I tried calling Ned. His phone rang and rang before finally going to voice mail. I sent him a text in case he woke up and checked his phone, but I didn't wait for a call back. I quickly changed out of my pajamas and threw on a jacket and sneakers. I took my phone, my car keys, and the chalk bag I'd found, left a note on the breakfast bar for Hannah and my dad, then ran out to my car in the early morning darkness.

The streets were quiet, and I arrived at Ned's in record time. Bess and George weren't there yet. Ned's house was dark, and I noticed his car wasn't parked in the driveway as usual, but that wasn't necessarily cause for alarm; he could've parked in the garage.

While I couldn't see into his room from where I'd parked, I'd be able to spot anyone approaching the window or climbing out of it. I waited in my car with the lights off, keeping my eyes peeled. After a few minutes, I texted George: Where are you?

Sorry, she replied. Got caught up w/Biblioghost shutdown. Leaving now!

Knowing George, that meant they'd be another fifteen minutes at least. I turned on the radio at a low volume to keep myself from nodding off, and it wasn't long before I realized I recognized the voice speaking. It was Terry Vila, in the middle of another rambling *Tales from the Haunted Library* monologue. I didn't realize his show was broadcast on the radio, but then, I'm usually not listening to the radio at this hour.

"You've been listening to *Tales from the Haunted Library*, broadcasting live on air for the first time. That's right, listeners, this old bat left his underground lair and made the leap from podcasts to the big time, with a special six-hour marathon show. Welcome to our cursed carnival! Prepare yourselves for the unholy truth. . . ."

That explained why Terry wasn't around to capture the intruder currently treating Coffin Hall like her own personal catwalk.

"The time is five twenty-seven a.m. We'll bring on our next special guest soon. Remember, it's still the witching hour, so keep your wits about you. And now, a word from our sponsors."

A silky female voice came over the speakers. "Coughlin Capital welcomes you to schedule a tour of our brand-new luxury development, opening next year! The fabulous Coughlin Cooperative will feature two-bedroom condominiums, complete with top-of-the-line fixtures, en suite Jacuzzis, home gyms, a fabulous rooftop lounge, and on-site boutique shopping. Sign up today to be placed on the waiting list! Coughlin Cooperative: Modern homes for modern people."

I shook my head in disbelief. Terry was trying to play both sides, collecting his paycheck from Coffin Hall while raking in sponsorship money from the woman who wanted to destroy the library and everything it stood for. He probably had only shared our *Biblioghost* stream so he could make himself look like a big-time ghost hunter.

I now had proof that the Blue Lady was a fake and that Terry Vila was on Yvonne Coughlin's payroll, which meant he had a reason to look the other way in his second job protecting the library. Ned would be so disappointed. . . .

Just then Bess and George pulled up in George's mom's station wagon. I got out of the car, and Bess held up Harriet's diary.

"Do you want to hang on to this, Nancy?"

"Yes, I think it's safer to leave the diary in the car," I said. "I can lock it in my trunk." Bess agreed, and I noticed that her eyes were bloodshot.

"I've been poring over the symbols all night, and I haven't managed to decode a single word," she said dejectedly.

"If you ask me, this diary is a lot more trouble than it's worth," I said. "Why do you want to translate it so badly?"

Bess answered right away. "I feel for Harriet. She just wanted to be with the one she loved. But her father was too greedy to let her go. The whole thing is too sad. I can't let her story end that way."

I could understand Bess's point of view, but discovering who was behind all these break-ins seemed a lot more urgent right now.

Unfortunately, the most surefire way to wake Ned up was also the most obnoxious. I marched up to the entryway, my friends right behind me, and rang the Nickersons' doorbell.

Mrs. Nickerson came to the door in a robe after my third ring, yawning, her hair a bird's nest. "Nancy, what on earth are you doing here at this hour? And—is that George and Bess? Girls, is everything okay?"

"I'm sorry, Mrs. Nickerson. Normally, I would never bother you so late—er, so early. But we think Ned might be in danger. Someone broke into my room tonight, and I'm worried the same person—or one of their accomplices—is going to come after Ned, too. Can we just check on him?"

"Someone broke into your room? Nancy, you should be talking to the police right now, not driving all over town waking up your friends."

"I know, but if I try to explain everything, they won't believe me. Please, will you let me peek into Ned's room? It would make me feel so much better. Then we'll get out of your hair, I promise."

"Go ahead, but I don't think there's anything to worry about. I haven't heard a peep out of him all night. I can't promise his room is presentable. I'm going back to bed, so you girls can let yourselves out when you're satisfied that my son is alive and well. After that, I hope you'll go straight to the police station."

"Okay, thanks, Mrs. Nickerson. And sorry again to wake you," I said meekly.

She just grunted and shuffled back to her bedroom.

I tiptoed down the hall toward Ned's room, followed by Bess and George. I knocked, then listened at the door for a second, and when I didn't hear anything, I went in.

The room was dark and chilly, and to my dismay, Ned's window was wide open. His bed was empty, the covers thrown back as if he'd jumped out in a hurry, and his phone had been left behind on the nightstand. The lock screen was filled with notifications about my texts and voice mails.

"Oh no," Bess murmured.

George said, "Ned, whatever prank you think you're pulling right now is *not* funny. Come out, come out, wherever you are!"

She ducked under his bed and checked the closet, but the room was empty.

Instead of bursting into tears and calling for Ned's parents, I went to the open window and examined the frame and windowsill. I didn't find any scraps of fabric or smears of paint, and the ground under the window was undisturbed. Ned wasn't a sleepwalker, and as far as I knew, he didn't have any reason to leave his home in the middle of the night, especially not without his phone. Had he gone of his own free will, or had someone taken him?

I left Ned's room and found the door to the garage. Inside was only his dad's tool bench, the washer and dryer, and the family SUV. So Ned could have driven himself. But where was he going?

Bess asked me what I wanted to do. I didn't know. I felt more lost than ever, and now Ned was missing. I needed a minute alone, so I told my friends I was going outside to think. Bess kindly offered to wake up Ned's parents and break the news.

Outside, an early morning chill had set in, so I got into my car to warm up. When I turned the key in the ignition, the radio came on again, and I realized I recognized the voice of the man who was speaking to Terry Vila.

It was Ned.

"I didn't have anything to do with the *Biblioghost* hoax, and I did not steal Harriet Coffin's diary!" Ned objected.

"That's not what my sources say," Terry replied smoothly.

"That's pretty rich, Terry, considering it's your actual job to protect Coffin Hall from intruders!" I shouted at my radio, forgetting that Terry was in a studio somewhere and couldn't hear me. I wasn't going to let Terry have the last word. I was going to find his new broadcast studio, and I had one good guess where it was. Taking Yvonne's classy business card from my wallet, I typed the address into the maps app on my phone. It was a twenty-minute drive from Ned's house.

Over my speakers, Terry was explaining that he personally had checked the tower room for Harriet's diary after the fire. "And wouldn't you know it, I found the case empty. Who was the last person seen in the tower room? That's right, it was *you*, Ned Nickerson. You stole Harriet's diary!"

I could tell Ned was blindsided. Instantly, he lost all his usual cool.

"N-no, that's n-not what happened!" he stuttered. "I—I was s-saving it!"

I wasn't going to leave Ned to defend himself alone. I had to get to Terry's radio studio, and fast.

I burst back into the Nickerson house and found Bess and George sitting with Ned's parents at the kitchen table.

"Ned's okay," I told them. "He's giving an interview on a radio show. There's not really time to explain. But everything is fine. I'll pick him up and bring him home to you in time for breakfast. Well, better make that brunch. We have some debunking to do."

Ned's mom gave me a puzzled look but didn't ask any questions. "Okay, I trust you, Nancy. As long as you're around, I know my son will be safe. I'll make French toast," she said, and gave me a peck on the cheek.

CHAPTER TEN

~

The Missing Boyfriend

BESS AND GEORGE AGREED TO CARPOOL with me, and the three of us piled into my hybrid. Bess conked out a few minutes into the drive, followed by George. They had been up all night, poring over that dingy old book and those camera feeds. They deserved a little rest. Even so, I kept Terry's show on at a low volume. He had started taking calls from his listeners. Not a single caller came to Ned's defense—they all agreed that Ned had been behind the Blue Lady hoax all along and said he'd obviously stolen Harriet's diary. The callers offered theories about where he could be hiding it and what his possible motives might be. Ned could barely get a word in to defend himself.

My mind was racing. I had to find a way to turn Terry's interrogation around on him and prove that Yvonne Coughlin was the real mastermind behind these fake ghost sightings. Luring Terry away from his security post at Coffin Hall with money and a brand-new studio certainly looked suspicious, but it wasn't exactly evidence of any wrongdoing.

We parked directly in front of the Coughlin Capital offices, a glass-and-chrome building with an ugly abstract sculpture out front that looked like a dollar sign made of knives. Downtown River Heights was just waking up. Baristas and bakers and grocery store cashiers and news clerks were chaining up their bikes and turning on lights, receiving deliveries, and getting ready for the day. A few early risers were out walking dogs or jogging as the sun peeked over the horizon.

George found a way to connect her laptop to the Coughlin Capital Wi-Fi network (don't ask me how). She showed me the handful of useful reports that had come through before the viewers turned on us—a few screenshots where the Blue Lady's shadow was clearly visible, one where I could see the tip of her shoe poking out from under her glowing skirt, and one where I could make out the imprint of a face under the veil.

George also pulled up another shot from later in the night, more than an hour after the decoy Blue Lady made her appearance in the library's lobby. In it, an odd bluish blur could be seen at the entrance to the tower stairs. George pointed out a small patch of light over the railing that she thought might be the Blue Lady's hand—the *real* Blue Lady. I told her it was probably Photoshopped or some webcam glitch.

Regardless, I told her to send me the best evidence before I went into the studio. I'd need every bit of proof I could get.

A bright blue smart car pulled into the Coughlin Capital employee lot and parked near the side entrance. The driver was a tired-looking young woman with blond hair tied up in a complicated twist. I told George to stay in the car with a sleeping Bess while I scoped out the situation. Closing the door quietly, I slowly approached the stranger's car, giving a little wave and smiling widely as I rapped on her window. The young woman rolled it down a couple of inches and looked at me with wide, frightened eyes.

"Hey! Sorry," I said. "Are you the new intern?"

"Yes! Hi! My name's Carrie Ann. Sorry, were you expecting me? Did I keep you waiting?"

Lucky guess, Drew, I thought.

"I'm sorry I'm late!" she continued. "I know Ms. Coughlin said to be here at six a.m. sharp, but I slept through my alarm and then my boyfriend's lizard got sick. I'm sorry!"

"Nice to meet you, Carrie Ann, I'm Nancy Drew," I said, extending my hand through her open window. "I hope your boyfriend's lizard is okay. And you have nothing to be sorry about. I don't work for Yvonne. I'm actually supposed to be a guest on the radio show this morning. Could you show me the entrance to the broadcast studio?"

"*Phew!* Honestly, I'm just glad I'm not in trouble. I

started here a couple of months ago, and I can't seem to stop making mistakes. I've never had an internship like this one. Ms. Coughlin's a pretty, ah, unusual boss. She expects a *lot* from her employees."

Carrie Ann opened her door and climbed out, unfolding her long legs and standing to her full height, which had to be at least six feet. I couldn't help but notice the resemblance to her boss.

"Sorry, did you say you're here about the radio show?" she asked. "I can't believe anyone's listening to that."

"I'm not exactly a fan," I answered, "but I need to make an appearance. Could you let me in?"

"Technically, the offices don't open until six thirty," Carrie Ann said. "I'm just supposed to be here before everyone else to make the coffee."

"I won't be any trouble. I'd ask Terry to let me in, but he's not answering his phone."

Carrie Ann shrugged. "Sure, why not." She opened her trunk to remove a large black garment bag, which was only partially zipped. Part of the garment inside slipped out, and I could see it was a 1920s-style flapper dress with the same dropped waist and beaded fringe I'd seen on the dress in Harriet Coffin's portrait, but this fringe looked weirdly shiny, like plastic, and this dress was white, not blue.

"That's pretty," I said. "What is it made of?"

"I think it's called fiber-optics? The dress actually lights up! But it also itches like crazy. This is one dress I don't mind returning. Honestly, I don't know how much longer I want to keep doing this internship. It's all a bit too much for me. . . ."

I wanted to ask her to say more, but I was a little dumbstruck by the Coughlin offices. We stepped through the smoked-glass doors into a long white hallway decorated with more gaudy abstract sculptures and black-and-white photographs of Yvonne Coughlin posing in haute couture with expensive cars, lavish pools, saunas, and other luxury features of the company's development projects. She looked different in every photograph, transforming her face with dramatic makeup and hairstyles to complement each setting.

The hallway ended in a large open-plan office done in pinks and golds, with lots of giant potted plants that on closer inspection turned out to be fake. I noticed that none of the desks had chairs—they were all set high off the ground so employees would have to stand to get anything done. Carrie Ann led me to a seating area at the far end of the room, across from an imposing set of double doors that I assumed led to the executive offices.

"Can I get you coffee, tea, seltzer, kombucha, cold pressed juice, bee pollen, nut milk, a shot of turmeric, or a bottle of imported Icelandic lava water?" Carrie Ann asked.

"Uh, no thanks, I'm good. Where's Terry's studio?"

Carrie Ann frowned. "I'll show you where to find him. Though I don't exactly recommend it. That guy never stops talking." She flung open the double doors and pointed down the carpeted, softly lit hallway. "He's at the end. Third door on your left."

There was a flashing red light above the door-frame. Bingo! Radio studios used lights to signal that they were on the air and shouldn't be disturbed. At the door, I peeked through the double-paned glass at Terry's new lair.

Ned and Terry sat on opposite sides of a large silver microphone on a desk in the middle of a large windowless room. Both wore large black headphones with curly wires attached to a sound panel on Terry's side of the desk. The walls and ceiling were covered in squares of nubbly black foam, and there was a bank of computer monitors to Terry's right, showing the live feed of Terry and Ned's audio levels. I knocked on the window and tried the handle, but the door didn't budge.

"Don't bother!" Carrie Ann called to me down the hallway. "It locks automatically when he's on the air. And it's soundproof, so they won't hear you."

"Oh, rats! When do you think I can get in there?"

"There will be a commercial break soon, I'm sure. Terry's contract says he has to plug Coughlin Capital every so often. Good luck!" With that, Carrie Ann gave me a halfhearted wave and shuffled off to the coffee station.

The studio lock was digital, so I wouldn't be able to pick it. I'd have to wait for the commercial break. Pressing my ear against the door, I could just make out Ned speaking quickly and passionately, the way he did when he was arguing with my dad over some case detail.

Frustrated, I paced to the end of the hallway past the sitting area with its empty receptionist's desk, and stopped in front of the door marked with a gold plaque that read YVONNE COUGHLIN, SHE-EO. Underneath the words was an elegant engraving of a swan.

On a whim, I tried the door.

Locked.

Fortunately, I always carry a bobby pin or two, and this door had a much simpler mechanism than the studio one. After a little jiggling and a *pop*, the door swung open, and I was inside Yvonne Coughlin's inner sanctum.

The office was carpeted in pale pink plush carpet, and all the furniture was curved and comfortable-looking, done in soothing pastel shades. Yvonne's desk was made of clear Lucite, and instead of an office chair, she had a huge throne upholstered in white satin. She had her own en suite bathroom, too, and what looked like a walk-in closet. But I wasn't here to marvel over Yvonne's luxurious lifestyle.

There was a report open in the middle of her desk. Of course, I peeked. Two columns labeled *Adverse Possession* and *Hostile Possession* were followed by dense legal language that I couldn't make heads or tails of. There was a pink Post-it attached to the top page with the words *CH Strategy!* written in spiky letters. I snapped a picture with my phone and texted it to my dad, followed by the message: Could you please translate this into plain English for me?

There was only one photograph on Yvonne's desk, what looked like a party scene. Two women in tiaras had their arms wrapped around each other, their faces lit up. The woman on the right was tall, blond, and— elegant—Yvonne, ten years younger, decked out in a minidress, vinyl boots, fake lashes, and sparkly eye shadow. The woman on the left was her opposite, athletic with not a trace of makeup, with close-cropped blue hair, dressed in jeans and a black motorcycle jacket. Despite their differences, the women were the same height, blue-eyed, and had similar noses. They looked very comfortable together.

In fact, they could have been sisters.

As I snapped a picture of the photo, I heard sounds on the other side of the door: employees greeting one another. I couldn't risk being caught snooping in the boss's office. I tiptoed to the door and opened it a crack.

The hallway was still empty, so I slipped out, locking the door from the other side before I closed it, and returned to the sitting area in time to watch the parade of Coughlin Capital employees coming in to work.

The first thing I noticed was that they were all women. Every employee was at least six feet tall, and not one of them would have been out of place at a fashion show in Paris or Milan. Each woman had expensively dyed blond hair and came dressed in the latest fashions: tailored pants suits and sheath dresses with killer heels in coordinated colors. They carried designer purses that probably cost more than my car.

A tall, muscular woman parted the crowd of chatty employees and came toward the sitting area. She was notably less made up than the rest and seemed to be wearing a fluffy blond wig, not her natural color if I could judge by the wisps of dark hair at her neckline. She was dressed simply in a navy-blue pants suit.

I said hello as she approached, but she ignored me and brushed past to the receptionist's desk just outside Yvonne's office doors. A nameplate on the desk read BRIDGET RICKETTS, EXECUTIVE ASSISTANT TO THE SHE-EO.

"Hi, Ms. Ricketts," I said. "I'm—"

"Nancy Drew, yes, I know who you are," she said, still smiling. "Yvonne told me you'd be stopping by."

"Uh . . . she did? Did she tell you why?"

"She told me you're a snoop. Is that true?" Ms. Ricketts's bright blue eyes bored into me.

"I like getting to the bottom of things, but I really didn't come here to snoop." I didn't have enough evidence to accuse Yvonne of anything—yet. "I actually came here as a guest of *Tales from the Haunted Library.*

My boyfriend Ned is in the studio with Terry right now—"

"Then I don't see what you would be doing in Yvonne's office. I saw you come out."

I blushed. "I'm sorry. I've been waiting awhile for the show to go off the air. I guess curiosity got the better of me. I just really admire Yvonne's, ah, unique style," I said, making a vague gesture at the glitzy office decor. When you're trying to get information out of someone, a little flattery never hurts.

"You don't have to lie to me, Nancy," Ms. Ricketts replied with a knowing smile. She leaned forward. "You suspect Yvonne of something."

"Of course not," I said quickly, worried that Ms. Ricketts would have me ejected from the building before I could get a chance to rescue Ned from Terry's questions. "I'm sure there's a perfectly good explanation for yesterday's events at Coffin Hall that doesn't involve Ms. Coughlin or her business."

"We have nothing to hide here," said Ms. Ricketts, with a shrug that struck me as a little too casual.

"People think Evie is a villain, just because she's rich and successful, but they don't see her heart. Do you know what she's been through these past few years?"

"What do you mean?"

"She lost her older sister, Isabella. Izzie was a talented actress, athlete, and poet. She spoke six languages. She died suddenly last year in a mountain-climbing accident in Alaska. Her body was never found."

"That's terrible. I'm really sorry for the loss. It must be so hard not to have any closure," I replied, but Ms. Ricketts waved away my condolences. She seemed more interested in dishing than grieving.

"Evie always looked up to Izzie, but Izzie never took her sister seriously. When Evie went into real estate, Izzie called her greedy and evil, and then she left for Alaska and never returned. I don't think Evie has gotten over it."

This secretary knew an awful lot about the Coughlin family's personal lives, and I couldn't help but notice how comfortable she seemed to be using their nicknames. Why was she telling me all this? It felt like a play for sympathy.

"Ms. Ricketts, you're here!" someone shouted excitedly. I looked up to see Carrie Ann, the front of her dress now covered in coffee stains, coming over to the secretary's desk. "I have some questions for you about the special project . . . you know, from last night?"

"Oh, Carrie Ann, uh, this isn't a good time—" Ms. Ricketts said.

"It'll just take a second, I swear," Carrie Ann protested.

"Fine. Follow me into Yvonne's office, so we can speak freely," Ms. Ricketts replied huffily.

I waited for the door to close behind them before peeking over Ms. Ricketts's desk at the black leather planner she'd left open to today's date. I carefully turned the page and examined Yvonne's schedule for the previous forty-eight hours.

I went over the timeline of ghost sightings in my mind. Yvonne's schedule showed that she had caught a flight to New York immediately after I'd seen her at the construction site, and that she wasn't due back until eight this morning. Despite the schedule evidence, I wasn't convinced. Yvonne had a reason to cause chaos at Coffin Hall.

I looked up from the planner just in time to see the light above Terry's studio suddenly blink out. They were off the air. Now I'd have a chance to defend my boyfriend in the court of public opinion.

CHAPTER ELEVEN

~

The Podcaster's Lair

I STEPPED INTO THE BROADCAST STUDIO and Ned let out a shout of surprise. He tore off his headphones, ran over, and flung his arms around me.

"Nancy, I'm sure glad to see you! I feel like a prize jerk for not telling you where I was going, and for leaving my phone at home," he said into my hair.

"It's okay. I know you were just starstruck," I replied, patting his back. "We'll find a way to talk you out of this mess."

Terry interrupted our reunion with a raspy "Hello?" He sounded tired and annoyed. He must have been talking for hours at this point. "Even though I don't remember issuing an invitation, it's an honor to welcome you to my temple of sound, Miss Drew. Our commercial break is nearly over. Why don't you pull up a chair and join us on air for the last few minutes? It's nearly time for the morning news."

I gulped but nodded. I'd never been on the radio before, and even if there weren't many listeners, it was still a little intimidating. I sat down and put on a pair of big black headphones, which blocked out the sound of the room so all I could hear was my own pulse.

Terry held up a hand and counted down from five.

"Welcome back, weary wanderers," he said into the microphone. "The Blue Lady, as I've been saying, is a hoax. We proved as much last night, thanks to my ingenious *Biblioghost* web camera security system. Ned Nickerson and his gang of fraudsters thought they fooled us with that ghost act in the main lobby, but many smart viewers pointed out that ghosts don't cast a shadow. Thanks to every listener who tuned in and sent us ghost reports."

"Wait a second—" I said, but Terry spoke over me.

"We've already heard about our friend Ned Nickerson and all the evidence that puts him at the scene of two Blue Lady sightings, during which precious volumes were destroyed and the historic rooms of Coffin Hall suffered considerable water and smoke damage. We also proved that Ned stole Harriet Coffin's diary from the library early yesterday afternoon. What we don't know is where he's hidden it, and so far, he refuses to tell us."

Terry was talking so quickly, it was impossible to get a word in edgewise. Every time Ned or I tried to interrupt, he just talked louder and faster.

"And now, loyal listeners, it's my pleasure to introduce a surprise guest! Ned's girlfriend, Nancy Drew, an amateur sleuth, is here live in the studio to tell us all about her role in the hoax."

I felt my phone buzz in my pocket, glanced down at the screen, and saw a message from my dad responding to my question about the document I'd seen in Yvonne's office.

Adverse possession = squatter's rights. It's a way to claim a property without buying it.

Reviewing the photo I'd sent, I noticed how similar the handwriting on the Post-it note was to the handwriting in Bridget Ricketts's day planner. Could *CH Strategy* refer to a plan to take possession of Coffin Hall? Why would Yvonne's assistant be advising her to steal land?

I didn't have time to think more about it because Terry was already firing off his questions in rapid succession.

"Nancy, was that you on the *Biblioghost* stream, dressed as Harriet Coffin? Were you Ned's accomplice? Why did you do it, and where is the diary now?"

Harriet's diary was currently hidden in the trunk of my car, protected only by an unconscious Bess and George, but I wasn't going to let Terry know that. Of course, I was going to speak up and defend myself and Ned, but I had to get the facts straight first.

"Hi, Terry. I'm happy to be here. Thanks for that . . . dramatic introduction. Can you hang on a second, though? I've just gotten some information that may help unmask the real criminals behind this hoax."

"Oh, by all means, take your time answering. . . . It's not like we're live or anything," Terry said with a sneer. "You know, the longer you hesitate, the guiltier you look."

Unfazed by Terry's radio-host bluster, I gave him my most charming smile. Then I took a deep breath and spoke clearly into the microphone, meeting Terry's gaze.

"I'm not the Blue Lady. But I think you know who's behind all this, and it isn't Ned."

"Is that so?" Terry said, arching one eyebrow.

"That's right," I said. "I'd like to address your listeners, if I may."

"Be my guest."

"Since you ghost hunters supposedly value the truth so much, let me ask you, did you know that this man, Terry Vila, has betrayed everything he believes in? Terry spent over a year of his life working security at Coffin Hall. He made his name in the podcast business telling stories about Harriet Coffin, the Blue Lady of Coffin Hall. And now, when Coffin Hall needs him most, he's abandoning the library and all its history. He was supposed to be on duty all night, but I guess he'd rather spend his time spreading conspiracy theories and spending Yvonne Coughlin's money. . . ."

Ned jumped in. "Terry, your response? How do you justify leaving your post?" Seeing me go on the offensive must have brought back his confidence. We do make a great investigative team.

"I wasn't going to pass up this broadcast," Terry said, waving away our questions. "Opportunities in radio don't come along every day, you know. With the webcams, I could keep an eye out for any funny business at Coffin Hall. No harm came to the library last night, so what's the problem?"

"Yesterday the library nearly caught fire *and* flooded," I countered. "And the Blue Lady made another appearance at four thirty a.m. How did you know that she wouldn't do any damage this time? The answer is you didn't. Unless you knew who was behind the ghost sightings."

"That's an interesting theory you have, Miss Nancy," Terry said. He was trying to play it cool, but I could tell he was shaken by the accusation. "But as you may know, on this show we rely on the facts. Do you happen to have any evidence that ties me to the Blue Lady hoax?"

"Your listeners want a grand finale, and I'm going to give it to them." Ned shot me a concerned look. He was right to worry. I'd barely slept, and my theory was still developing.

"Well, where is it?" Terry pressed.

I didn't have physical evidence tying Yvonne to the crimes at Coffin Hall. All I had were grainy screenshots, a disgruntled intern, a suspiciously powerful assistant, and a hunch.

My dad always says hunches are a shortcut, but there's no such thing as a shortcut when it comes to the truth. Truth comes with hard work and time. I didn't have time—Terry's show was already on the air. I'd have to go with my hunch.

"*She's* not an *it*. She's a person. But, oops, it looks like it's time for your next commercial!"

Terry groaned. "She's right, folks, it's time for another word from our generous sponsor. We'll be back after the break with more developments in the case of the Blue Lady of Coffin Hall." Terry held up one hand and counted down from five. "And we're clear. Ninety seconds until we're back on."

I nodded and ran out of the studio, nearly bumping into Carrie Ann, who was passing through the hallway.

"Just the girl I was looking for!" I told her. "I'd love to get a few sound bites from you on air about your experience working here. . . . Yvonne told me that was okay. She said you should feel free to speak truthfully."

Carrie Ann's face lit up at the invitation. "Oh yes, thank you for asking! Nobody ever asks me what I think."

"One more thing," I said. "Could you get that gown you showed me earlier?"

"Sure," Carrie Ann agreed happily. She skipped down the hallway and disappeared through a door, then returned with the garment bag in hand. I led her into the studio, sat her down next to Ned, and handed her a pair of headphones.

"Who are you?" Terry asked, annoyed that he'd lost control of his show.

"You don't recognize me?" Carrie Ann said. "I've been working here for six weeks. That's longer than you!"

Terry's screens flashed red and began counting down, and then we were back on air.

"Thanks for joining us for the radio premiere of *Tales from the Haunted Library*, where we're debunking the ghost sightings of Coffin Hall's famous Blue Lady!" I announced, before Terry had a chance to grab the mic. "Nancy Drew here. In defense of my boyfriend, Ned Nickerson, and the case of the *Biblioghost* hoax, I'd like to bring on a very special guest. Can you please introduce yourself?"

"Okay, um . . . Hi, everyone. My name is Carrie

Ann Bonner. I'm an intern at Coughlin Capital. But maybe not for long," she said, more quietly.

"Welcome, Carrie Ann. I'm glad you're here," I said, giving her a reassuring smile. "To start, would you tell the listeners how you came to work for Yvonne Coughlin?"

"When I moved back to River Heights last year, I wanted to volunteer at Coffin Hall, but after hearing all these spooky stories, I ended up applying for the internship at Coughlin Capital instead. My college counselor said I was lucky to get it—that Yvonne Coughlin had very high standards. But here I am. I must have something special, right?"

"I know you do, Carrie Ann," I replied. "I bet you'd be a great librarian, though. Don't give up on that dream."

"I've learned a lot about the business world."

"What have you learned so far?" I asked.

Terry crossed his arms and rolled his eyes, as if to say, *What does this have to do with anything?*

"Honestly, it's mostly spreadsheets, which aren't

so bad," Carrie Ann answered earnestly. "But I've also learned that being the boss means you can pay people to stand in for you when you don't feel like doing something."

I raised an eyebrow. "Has Yvonne ever asked you to stand in for her?"

"Yes, all the time."

"Can you give us some examples?"

"Oh, walking her dogs, picking up prescriptions or dry cleaning. Sometimes, meetings with clients she doesn't like. Even a blind date, once. I guess she got used to switching when her sister was alive, and she just hasn't stopped doing it."

"That's, um . . . not *not* shady," Ned said. "Carrie Ann, are you sure you want to say all this on air?"

"Yeah, I do," she replied. "I think I've had enough of being bossed around by Yvonne Coughlin and her assistant. Last night was the last straw."

"What happened?" I asked.

"Yvonne asked me to do something really weird. She said it was for work, but I'm not so sure. . . ."

"You can tell us," I said, giving her arm a little pat of encouragement.

Carrie Ann gnawed at her fingernail nervously, and when she spoke, the words came out all in one breath. "Yvonne's assistant called me in the middle of the night and told me to be ready outside my house in fifteen minutes. She said I was going to be the face of Yvonne's new marketing campaign, and then she drove me to the new construction site."

"Is that the site just outside Coffin Hall?" Ned asked.

"Yes."

"You said Yvonne's assistant brought you. Do you mean Bridget Ricketts?" I asked, remembering how much the assistant had known about her boss's personal history.

"Yes," Carrie Ann confirmed. "Yvonne is the brains and Ms. Ricketts is the muscle, even though she hasn't been at the company for long."

Terry leaned in toward his mic, getting ready to take over. I'd have to keep my questions coming and not let him get a word in.

"When did Ms. Ricketts start working at Cough-lin Capital?" I asked.

"A month ago. But she and Yvonne act like old friends."

"Last night, what time did Ms. Ricketts call you?" I asked. Across the table, I could see Ned putting two and two together, and I found I was smiling to myself. I do love to impress him with my investigative skills. Terry seemed intrigued too, despite himself.

"Around three fifteen a.m.," Carrie Ann replied, confident now. "We got out and Ms. Ricketts led me down into the excavation and behind a tarp into some sort of tunnel. I remember the ground was muddy at first, and we climbed a set of stairs and came up into a basement room with lots of pipes. Ms. Ricketts had me change into this gown—the one you saw me carrying this morning, Nancy. She also asked me to put chalk on my face and hands, but I said that would ruin my skin, so she gave me a veil to wear instead."

"That could explain the chalk marks I found!" I

exclaimed, pleased that I'd remembered to bring the bag into the studio with me.

"It's hard to be the face of something when your face is covered," Ned observed.

"Good point," I agreed. "Carrie Ann, tell them about the gown."

"I'm getting to that. I know it's radio, but can I show you guys something cool?" Carrie Ann asked, and held up the white gown. She reached deep into its skirt and must have flipped some kind of switch, because suddenly the plastic threads in the fabric lit up with a shimmering blue glow.

Ned leaned into the mic to speak to the listeners. "For those of you at home, Carrie Ann has produced an electrified evening gown that produces blue light . . . much like the one worn by the Blue Lady seen on our *Biblioghost* livestream early this morning."

"Fiber-optics, just like Bess said!" I exclaimed.

"I was so excited to get to wear something of Yvonne's. It's by a famous designer, you know. Ms. Ricketts led me up some stairs and pushed me into a pitch-black room with a high ceiling. She told me to pose and wave like I was in front of an audience, so I did. After a while, she came back, and we left. I was hoping Yvonne would come in today and explain it all to me, but after this whole experience, maybe I should quit instead. I'm starting to think that this internship isn't worth it."

"Yvonne really must think everyone lives to serve her," said Ned.

"You might be right about that," Carrie Ann said dejectedly. "Nancy . . . do you think I was part of this hoax you mentioned?"

"It seems likely. In fact, we have you on camera. Hang on, I'll show you." I pulled up the ghost reports on my phone, swiping through one photo after another. George had even sent me a clip of the Blue Lady swaying back and forth to music no one else could hear.

"That's me. That's definitely me," Carrie Ann said, her large eyes welling with tears. "Oh no, oh no, oh no. I'm in so much trouble."

As Carrie Ann was sharing her story, Terry had

been fidgeting in his seat, growing increasingly restless. His eyes darted between us and the monitors, as though he was calculating the number of people who had just heard his new boss exposed.

"You're not in trouble. Don't worry!" I assured Carrie Ann. "You didn't even know what Yvonne was up to. And you're not the only Coughlin Capital employee involved in this hoax."

Carrie Ann buried her face in her hands. Ned patted her back and offered her a tissue. Still, I wasn't finished with Terry.

"Terry, you must have known Yvonne would use Carrie Ann as a decoy. That's why you talked up the *Biblioghost* stream on your social media, and it's why you tried to blame Ned when the hoax was exposed. What was Yvonne trying to distract us from?"

Terry whirled around to the bank of computers and started typing frantically. The screens went dark, and I heard the crackly sound of dead air coming through my headphones. He'd ended the broadcast rather than fess up.

Carrie Ann took the opportunity to excuse herself. "If anyone sees me in here instead of out there working, Yvonne might actually bite my head off. Hope I don't get fired today, although maybe that wouldn't be the worst thing. Anyway, good luck, Nancy."

Ned and I hugged her and told her to keep her chin up, and then Carrie Ann left the studio.

I turned back to Terry, who was cowering in his chair as if he thought he could make himself invisible. "Well, what do you have to say for yourself?" I asked. Under the table, I took out my phone, opened the voice recorder app, and hit the red button, making sure to turn the phone so the microphone would capture Terry's voice. If he wouldn't broadcast his own confession, we could always release it as a special episode of *NED Talks*.

"I was trying to tell you earlier," he said. "It's impossible to make an honest living as a podcaster. I was in a tough place financially, and Evie offered me a lifeline."

Terry had used the same pet name for Yvonne that Ms. Ricketts had. Could they be more than just business partners?

"You didn't have to double-cross Miss Irene like this," I said. "Why didn't you tell her you were taking another job? Don't you think Coffin Hall deserves a little more respect?"

"All right, don't yell at me. I'm sorry!" Terry cried, holding up his hands. Off the air, he was just a meek little man with a lot of made-up stories.

"But it wasn't just about the money, was it?" I ventured, feeling bold. "Why are you protecting Yvonne?"

"You shouldn't meddle in family affairs," Terry replied, his once-booming voice now weak and wobbly. "I've been coming to Coffin Hall nearly all my life. I care what happens to that place. But I care about the Coughlin family too."

"Wait," Ned said. "Are the Coughlins related to the Coffins?"

"They're Harriet Coffin's first cousins twice removed," Terry replied.

"I knew the names were too similar to be a coincidence!" I said. "When you say it out loud, it's obvious."

Terry went on, "When we were growing up,

visiting the Blue Lady was something Yvonne and Iz and I did for fun. Sometimes, one of them would dress up in an old costume gown and hide in the stacks to frighten visitors. It was their way of connecting with their family history."

"Is that how this all started?"

"Okay, so, I might've let Evie into the library once or twice after Izzie passed away, when I was on duty, but I always kept an eye on her. I believed it was her way of mourning," Terry confessed miserably. "And I just can't say no to Yvonne. Her sister was the first friend I had here in town. It was the least I could do."

"Did Evie—Yvonne start the fire in the tower room yesterday?"

"Yvonne didn't have anything to do with that," Terry snapped. "Maybe she borrowed a few books and papers without Miss Irene's knowledge. Her methods are unusual, but she's writing her own destiny. Is that a crime?"

"It is, actually," said Ned. "You said it yourself: history can't be rewritten. The Coffin Hall collection belongs to the people of River Heights. Yvonne stole public property. That's what you accused *me* of on your show."

Terry sighed wearily, as if he knew we would never understand. "After Izzie died, Evie was the last living member of the Coffin family. She became obsessed with Coffin Hall. She says it's where she feels closest to her sister."

"If Yvonne loves Coffin Hall that much, why has the Blue Lady become so destructive?"

Terry's shoulders slumped and his face fell, as though somebody had let all the air out of him.

"I—I don't know. After the funny business with Hieronymous's portraits, and the time we found red ink splashed all over the map room, I confronted Yvonne and told her she had gone too far. She refused to apologize. She said the entire building and everything in it rightfully belonged to her and she could do whatever she wanted. I told her that was the end of her late-night visits, and I kept the doors locked from that point on. But unbeknownst to me, there was another way in."

"The tunnel," Ned said. "Is that how Hieronymous Coffin got water for his almond orchard?"

"Yes," Terry answered. "I'd read some cryptic mentions about a tunnel in Hieronymous's letters but never knew where the entrance was. After the flood yesterday, I went down to the basement and saw it for myself."

"Behind the pipes, right?" I interjected. "Let me guess . . . it was the weird metal door that Rosie said didn't lead anywhere."

"Miss Irene doesn't even know about it. Hieronymous planned the tunnel to double as an escape route, in case the townspeople ever turned against him," Terry went on.

"Where does that tunnel let out?" Ned asked.

Terry pursed his lips, refusing to respond, which was fine, because I already knew the answer.

"The Coughlin construction site. Isn't that right? The same site where I found this bag with the same chalk residue that was in the tower room and the Coffin Hall basement. The chalk and Carrie Ann's dress both lead us straight back to Yvonne Coughlin. Plus, she has a history of property damage in this very building. Do you still want to tell us Yvonne is innocent?"

"Like I said, the scary stuff, fires, floods . . . none of that is Yvonne." Terry wouldn't meet my eyes.

I looked at Ned, trying to figure out the best approach. "Let's say I believe you, Terry. Let's say Yvonne Coughlin wasn't the one who set the fire or started the flood. Who else would do something like that? Who would wish harm on the library, besides Yvonne?"

"I don't know."

"You don't know or you don't want to tell me?" I fired back. "Is there someone else pretending to be the Blue Lady?"

Terry hesitated. "I can't say."

"Why don't you want to answer my question?"

Fortunately for Terry, my phone rang. It was Rosie.

"You're supposed to keep it on silent in the studio," Terry muttered.

"Don't worry, we'll leave you to deal with your angry listeners," I said, standing up. "The library needs us."

As Ned and I left the broadcast studio, I heard the studio phone ringing off the hook. Then the door slammed shut behind us, the digital lock beeped, and the red light came on.

"Looks like Terry Vila talked himself into trouble," Ned said wryly.

A theory was coming together in my mind. All the evidence pointed to Yvonne: the chalk, the dress, her obsession with Coffin family history. But my instincts told me that Terry was actually telling the truth: she was innocent.

There was one other person who'd have the ability to pull off this hoax. The mountain-climbing, disguise-loving free spirit of the family: Izzie Coughlin.

According to everyone I'd spoken to, though, Izzie was dead.

Could a ghost impersonate another ghost?

CHAPTER TWELVE

The Ghost Unmasked

"NANCY, I'M SO SORRY," WERE ROSIE'S FIRST words when I returned her call. She sounded like she'd been crying.

"You're sorry? What for?"

"I didn't want to do it, but she was so angry with me. . . . She made me promise to do whatever it took to get it back—"

"Slow down, Rosie. Who was angry? What's going on?"

"Miss Irene! Terry called her last night to let her know he was quitting, and to make matters worse, he told her

Harriet's diary was missing, and that he was convinced you and Ned had stolen it. Miss Irene showed up at my house in the middle of the night and said I had to help her find it, or else the library would be shut down and the Coffin estate auctioned off to the highest bidder."

"None of that is going to happen. The diary is safe. We've been taking good care of it. And we were always going to give it back."

"*I* know that, but Miss Irene wouldn't listen to anything I said! She drove me to your house and told me to climb through your window. I knew it was wrong, but I felt like I didn't have a choice. Please don't hate me!"

"Oh, Rosie, I don't hate you. In fact, I like you a lot!" I assured her. "And I can forgive Miss Irene for overreacting. So that was you in my bedroom in the fancy nightgown and the clogs?"

"I like to dress up for bed, like a vampire," Rosie replied, regaining a bit of her dramatic flair.

"Where are you right now? I've learned some things about the Blue Lady that might change Miss Irene's outlook on this whole situation."

"I'm at the library, of course, mopping up the rest of the mess from yesterday. Miss Irene's holed up in her office. She won't speak to me."

"We're on our way now. Harriet's diary will be safe in Miss Irene's hands in thirty minutes."

"Thank you, Nancy. I'm sorry again, a thousand times. I owe you for life!"

I laughed. "No problem. I forgive you. In a weird way, I'm glad you were the intruder and not some stranger—or worse, Yvonne Coughlin. But Rosie, could you do me a favor?"

"Anything," she said.

"Next time you want to come over, text me first."

"Ha! Will do, Nancy Drew," Rosie said before hanging up.

Ned and I left Coughlin Capital and got into my car with Bess and George. Bess woke up and demanded to stop for iced coffee, but I told her if she could hold out until we returned Harriet's diary, Ned's mom was making French toast with extra whipped cream.

Ned caught my friends up on what had happened in the studio while I focused on the road. Even though I'd made the journey to Coffin Hall three times in less than twenty-four hours, this time the drive felt twice as long. I ran through the whole case out loud. It always helps me to bounce ideas off George, Bess, and Ned. Where would a detective be without her squad?

"Okay, so Rosie's confession solves the mystery of my midnight intruder. But the motives behind this Blue Lady hoax are still murky. I know Yvonne Coughlin is involved somehow, but so far I haven't been able to pin her at the scene of any crime."

"We know Yvonne isn't above hiring people to stand in for her," Ned reminded me. "Carrie Ann obviously didn't start the fire or cause the flood. Who could have done it?"

"Terry is partly to blame. . . . He may not have been directly involved in any criminal activity, but he's an accomplice, and too close to Yvonne Coughlin for his own good," I answered, making Ned wince. I could sympathize. It's not easy to see your idol sell out.

"Nancy, do we have to return Harriet's diary to that mean librarian right now?" George pleaded. "We haven't cracked the code yet, but I know we will soon!"

"Miss Irene isn't mean, she's just stressed out," Bess insisted. "Put yourself in her position. Would you want to be the person responsible for a whole building full of precious books?"

"No, thanks," George replied with a chuckle. "I can't even keep a plant alive."

"Exactly. And we already scanned the entire diary, so we don't really need the original anymore," Bess reasoned. "If we give it back to Miss Irene, I'll have an easier time convincing her to let us study the rest of William's letters to Harriet. There's got to be a key written down somewhere."

"Love the can-do attitude, Bess," I said, "but I want to point out that Miss Irene did order her volunteer to break into my house in the middle of the night, which is a little bit mean, and a little bit suspect. Could Miss Irene be in on the hoax? Rosie did say that she didn't want to do anything about the ghost at first and that she only hired security after the board found out about all the break-ins."

In my rearview, I saw Bess shake her head. "No. More than anyone, Miss Irene has dedicated her life to that place."

"But what if Miss Irene has had enough of the responsibility?" I suggested. "She could be persuaded to team up with her nemesis if they had a shared goal."

"I don't know, Nancy," Ned said. "I don't see Miss Irene getting involved with Yvonne Coughlin for any reason. Rosie said she fought against Yvonne's offers to buy the estate. Why would they secretly be in cahoots?"

I couldn't think of a good reason, and I was still uncertain that Yvonne had actually caused the mayhem at Coffin Hall. From what Terry had told us, she had a genuine interest in her family history. Why would she suddenly decide to destroy her ancestral home? It didn't make sense.

Up ahead, I saw the corner of the wrought-iron fence that marked the entrance to the estate, and beyond that, the yellow metal arm of an earthmover protruding from the Coughlin Capital construction site. As we turned onto the driveway, I noticed a beat-up truck parked near the chain-link fence. Beside the truck was a brand-new spotless white convertible with leather seats, parked at an odd angle, as though the driver had pulled up in a hurry. I rolled down my window to get a better look and caught the scent of something burning on the wind. A column of gray smoke curled skyward from the dirt pit where Yvonne planned to build a parking garage.

"Hang on, I'm pulling over," I told my passengers. "There's a fire at the construction site!"

We climbed out of my hybrid and approached the site slowly. Ned took my hand and Bess took George's. As we got closer, I saw light blaze from under a tarp at the far side of the excavation. A wave of intense heat hit me, and I realized whatever was behind the tarp was on fire. Nearby, two tall figures were in the middle of a heated argument. The figure on the left was Yvonne Coughlin, wearing a lime-green jumpsuit with a shiny sun visor flipped up over her forehead. The figure on the right was a dark-haired woman who looked familiar, and she was waving something over her head. . . .

"Is that Bridget Ricketts? What could she be up to?" I wondered out loud.

Suddenly Bridget grabbed the tarp and pulled it down, exposing the mouth of a large tunnel, leaking smoke. A snaky line of smoldering material at the bottom of the tunnel led the flames away from the entrance into darkness.

Yvonne screamed, yanked the tarp away from Bridget, and attempted to rehang the sheet to cover the tunnel entrance, but it was no use.

"That must be the tunnel Terry and Carrie Ann were talking about!" I exclaimed.

"So *that's* Yvonne. She looks scary," Ned said, sounding terrified.

"Are you kidding? She looks fierce! What a fab jumpsuit," Bess replied. "I think it's Versace. . . ."

"Guys, let's not get distracted by fashion while

something is on *fire*," George reminded us. "That's a lot of smoke."

I tried hollering and waving my arms over my head to get Yvonne and Bridget's attention, but they didn't seem to notice us. Meanwhile, the clouds of smoke grew thicker and blacker as the fire smoldered deeper into the tunnel.

"That's it, I'm going down there," I announced. I slipped along the gravel drive into the excavation pit, followed by George and Ned, with Bess reluctantly bringing up the rear. As we got closer, I noticed a wheelbarrow behind Bridget, filled with straw and a pile of rectangular red canisters. They had long black nozzles, like gasoline cans, and suddenly I understood why neither woman seemed to be trying to put out the fire. They'd started it, fueling the blaze with straw and gasoline. They seemed to be using the tunnel as a fuse, letting the fire rage underground straight toward Coffin Hall.

Yvonne Coughlin spotted us first, and the blood drained right out of her face as if *we* were the ghosts.

"Yvonne! Ms. Ricketts! What have you done?" I demanded.

"Nothing we aren't entitled to do," Ms. Ricketts snapped.

"Nina, this isn't the best time," Yvonne called. "We're having a family discussion, if you hadn't noticed. It's rude to interrupt."

"The name's Nancy," I shot back. "And if *you* hadn't noticed, there's a fire happening right beside you. Maybe we should do something about that first?"

"I'll call the fire department," Ned offered.

"That won't be necessary," Ms. Ricketts replied coolly. "There's nothing worth saving here."

"What do you mean?" I asked, more than a little distressed by the flames I could see licking the roof of the tunnel.

"I'm gonna call them anyway," Ned said quietly, sneaking away to dial.

"As the true inheritors of the Coffin Hall estate, we've decided it's more trouble than it's worth," said Ms. Ricketts.

"*We* haven't decided anything!" Yvonne snapped.

The smoke was making my eyes water and my throat feel scratchy. "Why don't you come over here, away from the smoke, and tell me more," I suggested. The blaze in the tunnel burned brighter as Yvonne and Ms. Ricketts picked their way across the site. We didn't have much time.

"Hang on, did you just say you're one of the inheritors of Coffin Hall?" George interjected. "I thought you were a secretary!"

Ms. Ricketts let out her barking laugh. She wasn't acting like Yvonne's employee at all.

"She's not an assistant," I said, ready to test my theory. "She's Yvonne's sister, Isabella Coughlin, aka Izzie. Everyone thought she died. But you're not dead, are you?"

"You've got it, Nancy. I'm alive and well," said Izzie triumphantly.

"Wow, twist! Welcome back to the land of the living," Ned quipped.

"I know your family history is complicated, but

neither of you have a right to commit arson just because you feel like it," I said, crossing my arms.

"It's more than that," Izzie declared. "After my mountaineering accident, I was discovered by two Buddhist monks and nursed back to health in their community. The monks gave me a fresh start and a new outlook on life. I realized I couldn't stay tied to the past anymore. I gave myself a new name and a new haircut and came back to try and convince my sister to let go of her ties to the material world."

"When she showed up at my office a few months ago," Yvonne said, "I thought I'd seen a ghost! I can't believe you let me think you were dead for so long!"

"Sometimes, radical change comes with a cost," Izzie replied, unapologetic. "To be free from our family history, we have to make a sacrifice, and it's a big one. We have to put an end to Coffin Hall. That's what I was trying to show you with my raids of the tower room and yesterday's little fire. I never did find Harriet's diary, by the way. This, right now, is the grand finale. Then, we'll rebuild from the ashes."

"And people think I'm the dramatic one? You always take things too far, Iz!" Yvonne chided.

"When I care about something, I give a hundred and ten percent," Izzie argued. "If I have to become an angry ghost to get your attention, then I will!"

"I really missed you, you know," Yvonne said. "And I'm so glad you're not dead. But you can't just destroy our family estate!"

"I'm sick of talking about that stupid building!" Izzie shouted. "We've spent too much time fighting over it. It's time to give my sister and me a clean slate. That's why it has to burn."

Ned rejoined us and whispered to me that the River Heights Fire Department would be here in five minutes. I wasn't sure we could wait that long.

"Your sister is right," I said. "Arson won't solve your problems. Also, and this is important: it's a crime. You might think you're above the law, but I guarantee the courts won't agree."

"I just wanted to have a successful business and learn more about my family!" Yvonne lamented. "*She's* the criminal mastermind. I came here to try and stop her, but she just won't listen!"

"Maybe you're not quite as bad as your sister, but you shouldn't try to profit from your family's legacy, either. Harriet Coffin disinherited your ancestors for a reason. If you succeed in buying Coffin Hall and turning it into condos, you're disrespecting her wishes," said Ned.

"You know," George said, "if *I* were Harriet, I'd definitely haunt anyone who bought one of those stupid condos."

"Izzie, can't you see that this history is important to people besides your family, people like Miss Irene, Rosie Gomez, and Terry Vila?" Bess chimed in.

At the sound of Terry's name, Yvonne rolled her eyes. "That loser has had a crush on Izzie for years," she said. "When he figured out that Izzie was back and that she hadn't died, I had to give him his own radio show to keep him quiet."

"Why can't you be nicer to Terry?" said Izzie angrily. "He's been a good friend to both of us even when we weren't good friends to him."

While the sisters went on arguing, I decided to take the opportunity to address the fire in the tunnel, which was getting closer to Coffin Hall every second. I pulled out my phone and caught Ned's eye. He understood that I needed a distraction, and he and George and Bess started egging the sisters on, first taking Yvonne's side, then taking Izzie's.

Meanwhile, I dialed Rosie's number. She picked up right away.

"Nancy, what's going on? Where are you? I've been smelling smoke, but I can't figure out where it's coming from."

"Everything's going to be okay," I said, keeping my voice low so as not to distract the Coughlin sisters. "I just need you to do exactly as I say, okay? Don't let Miss Irene stop you."

"She's in such a bad mood, I don't think she'd come out of her office even if Coffin Hall was burning down."

"Let's hope it doesn't! Here's what I need you to do: Grab your toolbox and go back down to the basement where all the pipes are. Find the backflow preventer valve we turned on yesterday and switch it off."

"But Nancy, if I do that, the basement will flood again."

"Exactly. Once the water's rising, pry open that weird metal door behind the pipes and let the water flow through. If you do that, you'll save Coffin Hall!"

"Save Coffin Hall? What's going on? Nancy, you're scaring me."

"I'll explain later. Right now, I need you to do everything I told you, and hurry!"

"I'm on it! Here goes nothing. . . ."

I heard the wail of sirens, and a brigade of fire trucks appeared at the crest of the hill. Ned and George ran up the incline to wave them down.

"Looks like the show is over, Coughlin sisters," I said.

As firefighters swarmed the construction site, I heard a rushing sound, and a few seconds later, water flooded out of the tunnel mouth, extinguishing the flames.

Ned, Bess, George, and I gathered at the edge of the construction site, watching the Coughlin sisters being led away by two police officers for further questioning. Rosie had saved the library, and the hoaxers were finally in custody. Now there was only one thing left to do: return Harriet's diary to its place of honor in Coffin Hall.

Rosie and Miss Irene were waiting anxiously on the steps when we pulled into the parking lot. I held up the diary with an apologetic grin. Miss Irene let out a cheer, then self-consciously smoothed her hair.

"If I forgive you for breaking into my house, will you forgive us for borrowing Harriet's diary for one day?" I asked.

"I think that's a fair exchange," Miss Irene agreed. "Girls—and Mr. Nickerson—why don't you come to my house for tea and apology scones? Rosie, you too. At the very least, I owe you that and the morning off before we clean up from another flood."

"That sounds awesome!" exclaimed George, too excited by the mention of food to wait for the rest of us to answer.

"I can't wait to see Mr. Prettyfeathers again," said Bess happily. "Will you tell us more about William's letters to Harriet?"

"Yeah, there's got to be something in the letters that can help us crack Harriet's code," George said.

"I know I haven't been very good at accepting other people's help," said Miss Irene solemnly. "But I want to change that. What do you say we work together? Rosie can tell me what you've learned so far, and I'll share all my research with you."

Rosie beamed. "That's just what I've been waiting to hear," she said.

"All right, it's settled," I said. "Ned, you can tell your mom to stand down from breakfast duty."

"She'll be happy to sleep in." Ned chuckled.

While Ned called his mom, Rosie and I went up to the tower room together to put the diary back where it belonged.

I settled the journal into its display case. Rosie closed the case and locked it, then went to the door and started turning off the lights before heading down the stairs.

I lingered behind to take one last look at the grand room where Harriet Coffin had spent her childhood and young adulthood, surrounded by her books and William's letters. I hoped she found a way to make a life of her own in the outside world somewhere.

Though I knew there was no one else in the room with me just then, I thought I saw a glimmer of blue light among the dark stacks, but when I looked again, all was still.

"Rosie, is that you?" I called, but no one answered.

Too much ghost talk, I thought, laughing at myself. But as I slipped out of the room, I swear I heard someone whistling a jaunty tune somewhere in the stacks.

ROSIE, BESS, AND GEORGE WORKED together to crack Harriet's code and successfully translated her entire diary two weeks after Izzie and Yvonne Coughlin were arrested for attempted arson. Ned interviewed the codebreakers for his podcast episode, which was a surprising smash hit.

In her diary, Harriet laid out her plan to elope with her fiancé, William Bratt, and start a new life in California. Harriet had uncovered a plot by two of her cousins to declare Harriet incompetent and commit her to an institution so they could seize the Coffin fortune for themselves. Harriet vowed she'd never speak to her greedy family ever again, and she donated most of her fortune to charity. After our run-in with the Coughlins, I understand!

When the events at Coffin Hall made the news, the library got a flood of new visitors. _Biblioghost_ helped too. The city council decided to invest in turning the Coffin Hall grounds into a real public park with swing sets, picnic tables, public restrooms, and walking paths. Now the library is busier than ever.

Miss Irene finally hired Rosie as a full-time

employee, and Rosie was able to hire Carrie Ann as her assistant. Carrie Ann leads a weekly ghost tour through the old (reinforced) tunnel. She's great at doing spooky voices.

Yvonne was let go with a fine and community service, but Izzie had to spend a year on house arrest in River Heights, where she's rebuilding her relationship with her sister and her friendship with Terry Vila.

I'm glad Ned's name was cleared and Coffin Hall is a safe, welcoming place for readers again. I'm still skeptical about ghosts, but I guess I'm a little more open to the possibility. Sometimes, I even find myself whistling Harriet's tune. After all, you never know.